Praise for *The Sour Lemon Score* a

"Richard Stark is the Prince of Noir."

> Martin Cruz-Smith

"What chiefly distinguishes Westlake, under whatever name, is his passion for process and mechanics. . . . Parker appears to have eliminated everything from his program but machine logic, but this is merely protective coloration. He is a romantic vestige, a free-market anarchist whose independent status is becoming a thing of the past."

> Luc Sante, *The New York Review of Books*

"The Parker novels . . . are among the greatest hard-boiled writing of all time."

> *Financial Times*

"Elmore Leonard wouldn't write what he does if Stark hadn't been there before. And Quentin Tarantino wouldn't write what he does without Leonard. . . . Old master that he is, Stark does them all one better."

> *L.A. Times*

"The caper novel, the story of a major criminal operation from the point of view of the participants, has no better practitioner than Richard Stark."

> Anthony Boucher, *New York Times Book Review*

"No one can turn a phrase like Westlake."

> *Detroit News and Free Press*

The Sour Lemon Score

Parker Novels By Richard Stark

The Sour Lemon Score

RICHARD STARK

With a New Foreword by Dennis Lehane

The University of Chicago Press

The University of Chicago Press, Chicago, 60637
University of Chicago Press edition 2010

Printed in the United States of America

19 18 17 16 15 14 13 12 11   2 3 4 5

ISBN-13: 978-0-226-77110-6 (paper)
ISBN-10: 0-226-77110-5 (paper

Library of Congress Cataloging-in-Publication Data

Stark, Richard, 1933–2008.
  The sour lemon score : a Parker novel / Richard Stark ; with a new foreword by
Dennis Lehane. — University of Chicago Press ed.
      p. cm.
  Originally published: London : Fawcett, 1967.
  ISBN-13: 978-0-226-77110-6 (pbk. : alk. paper)
  ISBN-10: 0-226-77110-5 (pbk. : alk. paper) 1. Parker (Fictitious character)—
Fiction. 2. Criminals—Fiction. I. Lehane, Dennis. II. Title.
  PS3573.E9S68 2010
  813'.54—dc22
                              2009039135

⊚ The paper used in this publication meets the minimum requirements of the
American National Standard for Information Sciences—Permanence of Paper for
Printed Library Materials, ANSI Z39.48-1992.

Foreword

I had drinks with Donald Westlake once at a crime fiction conference in the winter of 2000. We talked mostly about two terrific scripts he wrote in the late eighties, one for Stephen Frears (*The Grifters*), the other for Joseph Ruben (*The Stepfather*), but we never discussed his alter ego Richard Stark or Stark's indelible creation, Parker. This would be less surprising if I weren't such a geek about the Parker books. I'd read them all in the summer of '86, (there were sixteen at that point.) Along with Elmore Leonard's work, they taught me nearly everything I know about how to execute violence on the page. As for Parker himself, he's a watershed character in American noir, nearly incomparable. So why didn't I fly my geek flag while hanging with the man who created him?

A sense of mystery, for one; I don't want to know too much about the artists who create the art that excites me. The collective dream that descends upon the reader of a fictional universe depends on believing that the dream is quite real, even while you know, of course, that it's not. I feared the more I learned about the mechanical strings behind Parker the more artificial he would seem. And finally, the writer is about the last person you should trust when it comes to interpreting his work. If we truly knew what we were doing, we probably wouldn't do it; it would feel too much like a straight job.

As to Westlake, himself, he matched my preconceived impression of the creator of the John Dortmunder novels—a wry, intelligent man, self-deprecating and steeped in irony.

Such was Donald Westlake. Richard Stark, however, was nowhere to be found. Because as playful as Donald Westlake is, Richard Stark is all business. Where Westlake's writing is chummy, Stark's is clinical. If Westlake is the guy you'd love to find sitting beside you at the bar on a raw March night, Stark is the guy you'd hope to avoid in the parking lot on your way home.

As a stylist, Richard Stark's sense of economy is surgical. He has no time for flatulent prose; one senses he holds the decorous in contempt. He evokes a world of medium-sized, nondescript cities or dusty flatlands. A lot of the action takes place in motel rooms, either the kind with wrought iron fire escapes right out the window or those "with concrete block walls painted green, the imitation Danish modern furniture, the rough beige carpeting, not enough towels." Like those motel rooms and like Parker, Stark is a model of efficiency. This isn't to say his style lacks amenities. The swift sentences move with a running back's fluid timing. He could no more be accused of soulless functionality than could Hemingway or Raymond Carver. Stark writes with economy, yes, and cold, cold clarity, but there's grace in the prose, a stripped-bare poetry made all the more admirable for its lack of self-consciousness.

And what did that cold clarity produce?

Parker. The greatest antihero in American noir. If Parker ever had a heart, he left it behind in a drawer one morning and never came back for it. He never cracks a joke, inquires about someone's health or family, feels regret or shame or even rage. And not once in the sixteen novels that comprise the FPE (First Parker Epoch, 1962–74) does he wink at the reader. You know the Wink. It's what the "supposedly" amoral character does to let the reader know he's not *really* as bad as he seems. Maybe, in fact, he's been the good guy all along.

Parker *is* as bad as he seems. If a baby carriage rolled in front of him during a heist, he'd kick it out of his way. If an innocent woman were caught helplessly in gangster crossfire, Parker would slip past her, happy she was drawing the bullets away from him. If you hit him, he'd hit you back twice as hard. If you stole from him, he'd burn your house—or corporation—to the ground to get his money back. And if, as in *Butcher's Moon*, the sixteenth of the sixteen FPE novels, you were stupid enough to kidnap one of his guys and hold him hostage in a safe house, he would kill every single one of you. He'd shoot you through a door, shoot you in the face, shoot you in the back and step over your body before it stopped twitching.

Nothing personal, by the way. He gets no pleasure from the shooting or the twitching. He's not a psychopath, after all, he's a sociopath. But first and foremost, he is a professional. He's the progenitor of many a fictional criminal antihero, but those progeny are always redeemed by a need to connect with the human race. James Ellroy's antiheroes come immediately to mind, and it's hard to think of a more resolutely scumbag act than the protagonist of *White Jazz* throwing a mentally handicapped man out a window in chapter one. Yet by chapter thirty, he's reached out to the reader along the lines of shared humanity, and he's garnered our empathy, if not our love. Similarly, in the films of Michael Mann, many of the protagonists, from Frank in *Thief* to Dillinger in *Public Enemies*, share Parker's emotional retardation and consummate professionalism, but in that very professionalism Mann finds nobility. Cop Vincent Hanna in *Heat* clearly admires the work ethic of criminal Neil McCauley, while Frank in *Thief* asks the cops who shake him down why they don't try, as he does, to actually work for a living. But in the moral universe of the Parker novels, the very idea of nobility is laughable—Parker *is* a sociopath. The world he inhabits, however, is worse.

It's a world of absolute rot. Nothing and no one is above it and most are happiest that way. The Outfit sits atop a pyramid comprised of luckless thugs, idiot muscle, hustlers, grifters, hookers with hearts of bile, and bloody avarice so banal yet so all-encompassing as to wallpaper every room in every scene of every one of the sixteen Parker novels. The Outfit casts its shadows everywhere. It's the grimy engine that runs the grimy car with the faulty brakes and the crap transmission, yet when the brakes blow and the transmission seizes, the Outfit tells you it's your fault. And your bill.

Who can fight against this? Not the hero with the heart of gold. Not the Nice Guy or the Good Guy or the Morally Compromised But Ultimately Nice Good Guy. No. Only a cog in the machine can screw up the machine. A piece of the machine as grimy and hard as the rest of it. A chunk of steel. Or pipe of lead.

Parker is the lead pipe. He has no illusions about the machine—not a single ideal left to shred or a romantic notion left to dispel. Like the machine, he is heartless. And this is where he differs from every other antihero in noir. James Ellroy's protagonists have heart, however deeply buried. Jim Thompson's characters might not have heart or sentimental notions, but they are ultimately punished for that lack. Same goes for James M. Cain's lecherous ids-run-amok. Hammett gave us Sam Spade, he of the physical resemblance to the devil, who finds his partner's killer not out of noble principle but solely because it would be bad business not to. But while Spade may have no feelings for Archer, he is in love with Brigid O'Shaughnessy. Again, humanity creeps in whether the protagonist wants it to or not. This is a foundation brick of literary narrative—the antihero discovers his humanity, which allows us, the readers, to recognize ourselves in him and feel communion with the human race as a whole.

To which Parker says, screw that. Parker refuses to reveal his heart. Parker authentically and resolutely eschews sentiment. Or emotion. Parker never asks for understanding or grasps for a common cord between himself and the reader. (If the common cord held monetary value, he'd steal it. Otherwise, it's all yours.) What Parker represents, at least to me, is the abolition of the wish fulfillment that forms the firmament of narrative literature, a firmament I, myself, usually require, both as a reader and a writer. The wishes being fulfilled are familiar—good wins out, love conquers all, crime never pays, the check is in the mail. Well, in this case, the check *was* in the mail, but Parker intercepted it. And cashed it. And used it to finance a crime that paid double what you'll make this year.

So why do we like him for it? Why do we root for him? Why is it, after reading sixteen novels depicting the adventures of a heartless sociopath in the summer of '86, did I feel the desire for more? Why do I still look back on these novels, as a reader, with great affection and, as a writer, with wonder?

I still don't know the answer. Not absolutely. I *suspect*. I suspect we all recognize the Lie, even as we wrap our arms around it and hug it tight to keep us warm. The Lie is the illusion that we are safe, that we are watched over, that we will go gently and that the night is good. Not so, says Richard Stark. Not so, says Parker.

We are not safe. No one is looking out for us. And the night? The night is dark. So let's get to work before the sun comes up. Before someone catches us at it. Before the world wakes up.

Dennis Lehane

The Sour Lemon Score

ONE

One

Parker put the revolver away and looked out the windshield. The bank was half a block away along the sunny street. Andrews hadn't come out yet.

Next to Parker the driver, a man named George Uhl, rubbed his palms on the steering wheel and said, "What's taking him so long? Where is he?" It was a cool day, the temperature around seventy, but there was sweat on his forehead.

From the back seat Benny Weiss leaned forward and put a hand on Uhl's shoulder, saying, "Take it easy, George. Phil knows what he's doing; he's a good man. He's got to be sure nobody sees him do it, that's all."

Uhl nodded rapidly. "I'm just worried about the armored car," he said. "It'll be here and gone—"

"No, it won't, George. We've got a good five minutes. Relax, boy. Phil's a good man."

Parker listened to them, gauging them from the conversation. If Uhl was going to fall apart the whole operation was out the window. When Andrews came out of the bank they'd just turn around and drive away.

George Uhl was the only one Parker had never worked with before. A fairly young man of about thirty, tall and very thin and with receding black hair, he was Weiss's man, brought in and guaranteed by Benny, and that was why he worked so hard now to soothe Uhl and keep him calm.

Benny Weiss himself was always calm. A short man, stocky, his clothing generally as rumpled as if he'd just taken a cross-country bus trip, he'd been in this line of work thirty years now and was as excitable as a tailor facing a ripped seam. Parker had worked with him a few times over the years, and Weiss had always been solid, dependable and sure.

Still, Uhl was going to have to support his own weight. He was the driver and he had to be reliable. It had happened more than once in the world that a driver had gotten spooked and taken off in the middle of a job, leaving the rest of the string to dangle on a sidewalk someplace, loot in their hands and nowhere to go. So Parker listened to the other two talk, and considered scratching this entry right now.

Benny Weiss said, "Here he comes, George." He patted Uhl's shoulder. "See? Everything's okay."

"I see him," Uhl said. He sounded sullen, as though mad at himself for having gotten edgy. "I'm okay, Benny," he said.

"Sure you are," Weiss said.

Parker looked out through the windshield at Phil Andrews walking down the sidewalk toward the car. With the red wig and the sunglasses on, he was hard to recognize even when you knew it was him. Parker had watched him make himself up at the farm before they left, and it had been a good job, a subtle changing of the planes and textures of his face, using theatrical makeup in addition to the wig. When he'd finished he'd turned to Parker, grinning slightly, and said, "Meet my friend the bank robber." Because it was the face he put on before every job.

Phil Andrews was younger than Benny Weiss but had been a pro fifteen years at least, and the strange thing about him was that he'd never taken a fall. He'd never even been picked up on suspicion. The pro who never fell at all was the rarest of rare birds, and the reactions of other pros to Phil's streak took two extremes. There were those who wanted him in on every job they did, considering him good luck and a guarantee of safety for everybody else involved, which he wasn't; and there were those who refused to work with him on the grounds that he was overdue for a fall, the law of averages was going to have to catch up with him someday. As for himself, Parker didn't believe in luck, good or bad. He believed in nothing but men who knew their job and did it, and Phil Andrews was one of those.

He got into the car now, sliding into the back seat beside Benny Weiss, saying, "All set." He was the only one in any kind of disguise. The others all had prints and pictures on file and warrants out against them under one name or another. Being connected to one job more or less wouldn't make that much difference if they ever did get picked up.

Parker turned sideways in the seat, facing Uhl, so he could see everybody. "The question is," he said, "is George going to spook?"

Uhl looked at him in astonishment. "Me? Why?"

Weiss said, "Parker, of course not. George is okay."

Andrews said "What's wrong?"

Parker told him, "George was being nervous."

Uhl said, "You aren't nervous?"

"My face is dry," Parker said.

Uhl's hand went to his wet forehead. "I sweat a lot," he said. "It don't mean anything."

Weiss said, "Parker, a case of the jitters ahead of time, that's only natural. I get butterflies myself."

"I don't want to come out of that bank," Parker said, "and find no car."

Uhl said angrily, "What are you talking about? You think I'm an amateur, for the love of God? I've driven half a dozen times. I drove for Matt Rosenstein — you think *he'd* take a chance on somebody? You come out of that bank, I'll be right out front. Right in front of the armoured car, where we said."

Parker turned and looked at Andrews. Phil was studying Uhl's face. He met Parker's eye and shrugged. "It's just stage fright," he said. "I think he's probably okay."

Uhl gave him a belligerent grin. "I wouldn't want to bust your string," he said.

Andrews looked at him without humour. "That's right," he said. "You wouldn't."

Parker said, "Here it comes."

They looked out of the window and saw the dark blue armored car roll by. It pulled into the "No Parking" space in front of the bank, and two men got out of the cab.

Andrews said, "If we're going to do it, I've got to move."

Parker nodded. "Go ahead," he said.

Two

Parker was the last one into the bank. Andrews had gone first, getting out of the car again and walking down to the bank, going in just as two men in suits and with clipboards came out of the bank to meet the men from the armored car. They'd conferred out in the sunlight a minute, studying their clipboards, and then all four went inside again.

That was when Weiss moved. Getting out of the car, he clutched Parker's shoulder and muttered in his ear, "George is okay." Parker just nodded, and Weiss got out, shut the door, and went away to the bank, getting there just as the two uniformed armored-car guards came back out of the bank. There was a little mix-up at the door, and then Weiss was in and the guards were out. They went over and knocked on the rear door of the armored car.

Parker and the others had cased this one for three weeks and they knew the system cold by now. The coins went in first, in gray canvas sacks. The olive-green strongbox went last, carrying paper.

He watched the guard inside the armored car hand out the sacks of coins to the two outside. One of the men with the clipboards had hurried out after them and stood beside them now, pencil poised, checking things off.

The grenade was on the seat between Parker and Uhl. Parker patted it and said, "You remember how this works?"

"I'm all right now," Uhl said irritably. "I had a touch of the jitters. It never happened to you?"

"Never," Parker said. He opened the door and got out of the car and walked down to the bank. The guards had carried the coins in now, escorted by the man with the clipboard, and the guard inside the armored car had locked his door again.

Parker went into the bank. Weiss was standing at one of the

counters on the left wall, making out a deposit slip. Andrews was talking to the lone bank officer at the desks on the right, asking him about traveler's checks. There was nobody at the state lottery window in the far corner.

The guards came out of the vault area empty-handed, followed by the man with the clipboard. They walked past Parker and went outside again.

Three tellers' windows were open, two regular and the lottery window, all with female tellers. Two more female employees were at the calculating machines in back. Beside the clipboard men — one in the vault, the other outside with the armored car — and the bank officer to whom Andrews was talking, the only other male employee was the bank guard, an elderly man with a puffed-up pigeon chest and a dark blue uniform full of fold creases. His wife had ironed the shirt and folded it and put it away in a drawer, so when he took it out and put it on it had a checkerboard of creases all over it.

Parker stood looking around the room. It was a new bank with a low ceiling, which was good. There were only three straight customers in the bank, which was also good.

The two guards came back in, carrying the strongbox between them, one hand each. The clipboard man followed them, looking prissy and bored. Weiss crumpled up his deposit slip, put it in his pocket, and walked to the door. Parker went over to the bank guard and said, "Do you have a notary public here?"

His talking to the guard was the signal for Andrews to reach into his pocket and push the button on the little radio machine in there. Weiss was standing by the door, behind the armored car men and the clipboard man. If all was going right, Uhl was driving slowly down the block toward the bank right now, one hand holding that grenade.

The guard said, "Are you a deposi—" and the wastebasket by the lottery window blew up.

It was a huge noise, loud enough to give everybody in the bank a brief headache, and with it came a flash of yellow and white, and then flames were licking up the front of the counter toward the lottery window. On the heels of the explosion, one of the women employees screamed.

Parker had been standing so the guard's back was to the lottery window. At the explosion the old man spun around, startled, and Parker took out his revolver and clipped him with it behind the ear.

While the old man was still falling Parker spun around and held down on the two armored-car men. He shouted, "No heroes!" He knew Andrews had a gun on the bank officer and would quickly herd him into a corner away from telephones. He knew Weiss was behind the armored car men to let them know they were in a crossfire. And Uhl, at the sound of the explosion, was to drop the grenade out of the passenger-side window so it would roll under the armored car and was then to pull directly in front of the armored car and wait. In ten seconds, the grenade would start spewing black smoke. There wasn't much breeze today; the smoke would quickly billow out and surround the armored car and puff all around the bank entrance.

While Parker was shouting, Weiss was shouting also. Andrews was on his feet, waving an automatic and shouting at the employees, "It's a stickup! Don't move! Don't move!"

The armored-car men were professional enough to know when to fold a hand. Neither of them reached for a gun.

Parker said, "Put the box down. Now move over that way. Hands on top of your heads." He motioned the gun at the clipboard man. "You too."

"You can't —"

Weiss kicked the clipboard man in the butt. "Hurry up, shorty," he said. The clipboard man was about four inches taller than Weiss.

Parker and Andrews hurried over to the strongbox and each grabbed a handle. Weiss kept everybody covered. Parker went first, the heavy strongbox dragging him back, bumping into the back of his legs. He could see the smoke through the glass door, so Uhl was doing his job.

The smoke was everywhere, greasy and black, smelling of creosote. You couldn't see a thing, but Parker didn't have to see anything. He angled to the right, Andrews in his wake with the other end of the box, and they plunged through the smoke, Parker's hand out in front of him, till the heel of his hand hit the side of the car.

It took him a few seconds to figure out what part of the car he had, but then he moved quickly foward to the rear door, opened it, and clambered in with the strongbox banging against his heels. Andrews came piling in after it, and then Weiss rushed up out of the smoke, blundered the front door open, and jumped in.

Uhl burned rubber, taking off before either door was shut. For the first second or two he couldn't have been able to see a thing, but he tore out of the smoke as though God had told him personally there wasn't going to be anything in front of him, and there wasn't.

Everybody was done working now but Uhl, and Uhl had rehearsed his part so often he could almost do it asleep. Right at the corner, left at the alley halfway down the block, right at the next street, and then four blocks straight. They wouldn't hit a traffic light till then, and Uhl would be able to judge it from four blocks away and not have to stop for it. It was twenty minutes past ten in the morning, a dead time for traffic, so they'd be able to make any speed they wanted.

At that traffic light they'd make a left turn, and from there it was less than half a mile to the outskirts of town, where they'd stashed the other car. And after that a ten-minute drive to the farm, where they could hole up and wait for the fever to cool in the outside world.

Parker and Andrews straightened themselves out in the back seat, the strongbox lumping huge between them, leaning half on the seat and half on the floor. Andrews patted it, smiling, and said, "How much do you think?"

"Maybe forty," Parker said. "Maybe sixty. Maybe a little more."

"Not bad for a morning's work," Andrews said, forgetting the three weeks preparation.

Uhl, relaxed at the wheel now, glanced in the rear view mirror and said, "Shoot the lock off. Let's see how much it is."

"When we get to the farm," Parker said.

"Why not now?"

Weiss, up front with Uhl now said, "George, you want a bullet ricocheting around in the car? Where's your sense?"

"Oh, yeah," Uhl said, and made the right turn out of the alley. Four blocks away the light was red. Uhl drove at about thirty.

Parker turned his head and looked out the rear window. A couple of cars way back, moseying along. No pursuit. It would take them a while to get organized in all that smoke.

A siren. Everybody tensed, and then a police car shot across their path two blocks ahead, going from left to right, not slowing or anything. Everybody relaxed again.

Weiss said, "Going to the bank."

"Too late," Uhl said. "All the money's gone." The light turned green up ahead, and he accelerated.

Three

Parker kept one hand pressed flat on the strongbox. The last half mile to the farmhouse was over rutted dirt road, and the box tended to jounce. Parker said, "You can take it easy now."

"I'm anxious to know how much we got," Uhl said, but he slowed down some.

Everything had gone fine. The stolen car with its stolen plates had been abandoned behind the burned-out diner on the highway where they'd left the other car, this two-year-old Chevy, pale blue. They'd switched cars, carrying the strongbox over to this one, and then Uhl had driven sedately the rest of the way, never more than a couple of miles over the speed limit. One other police car had gone by, siren screaming, racing into the town they'd just left, but that was all the law they'd seen.

The farmhouse was gray, small, old, leaning, and weather-beaten. The porch roof was half fallen in, and only two window-panes were still unbroken. It stood on top of a bare hill, the dirt road passing at the foot of the hill and continuing on who knew where. Vague old grooves in the grass led upward to the right from the road, showing where another dirt road had once existed between here and the house. If you looked closely you could see where the grass had been recently mashed down by tires going up there, but the dirt road was seldom traveled and too bumpy to allow the people in a passing car to watch anything very closely. And at the top, around behind the sagging house, stood a sagging barn, big enough and empty enough inside for both this Chevy of Uhl's and Andrew's Mercury.

Uhl drove up the hill now, in low gear so the tires wouldn't leave skid gouges in the grass, and at the top he steered around the house and came to a stop in front of the barn. Weiss hopped out and dragged open the barn doors, and Uhl drove into the clammy, cool darkness inside the barn. He turned the key in the ignition and smiled over his shoulder at Parker and Andrews saying, "Home free."

"Maybe," Andrews said.

Uhl looked at him. "What's the matter? We're here, we're home free."

"We're home free," Andrews said, "when the last cop has quit looking and gone on to some other case."

"Oh, well," Uhl said, "if you're going to pin it down like that...."

"That's the only way to pin it," Andrews said. "You ready, Parker?"

"Ready."

They wrestled the strongbox out of the car and carried it across the strip of sunlight to the house. Behind them, Weiss and Uhl shut the barn doors.

Parker and Andrews carried the box into the kitchen. There were four chairs and a card table there, all brought up by Uhl and Weiss while provisioning this place. There was a pump at the sink, and it would still bring up water. Camping equipment was scattered throughout the house because they might be here for several days.

They put the box on the floor near the door while Uhl and Weiss came in, and Uhl went over and turned on their portable radio. They'd had the car radio on without yet hearing any report of the robbery, so this radio now played for them the end of the tune they'd been listening to in the car.

Andrews said, "Turn it down a little, George."

"Sure." Uhl turned it down, but then the announcer came on, gave the name of the record that had just played and then said, "This just in. The Laurel Avenue branch of the Merchants and Farmers Trust was robbed this morning of nearly thirty-three thousand dollars. In a daring daylight holdup, four men—"

"Thirty-three thousand?" Weiss looked tragic.

"Hush," Uhl said, and turned the radio up again.

The announcer had more to say, mostly in a daring-daylight-holdup vein, all the journalistic clichés pouring out, even finishing with the authorities confident of early arrests.

"They'd better arrest each other," Uhl said, grinning, and as another record started he turned the radio down again.

Weiss was gazing at the strongbox as though it had betrayed him. "Thirty-three thousand," he said. "A crummy eight grand each."

"We knew it could be low," Andrews said. "We knew it could be in the forty-thousand-dollar range."

"Range? You call that a range? It could've been in the *sixty*-thousand-dollar range, too! Fifteen thousand a man!"

"Eight thousand isn't bad," Andrews said. "Not for one morning's work."

This time Weiss wasn't going to let him forget the time spent in preparation. "What one morning's work? Three *week's* work, dammit, and a huge risk, a goddam huge risk, and for what? Eight thousand stinking dollars."

"I'll take your share, you don't want it," Uhl said.

"You shut up, George," Weiss said.

Andrews said, "Let's open it up. Who knows, maybe they counted wrong."

"They didn't count wrong," Weiss said, "and you know it. But go ahead, open it up. We might as well look at the damn stuff."

Parker opened the box with a hammer and screwdriver, and it took a while. In the meantime Uhl got cans of beer out of their portable refrigerator and opened them for everybody. Then they all sat around in the chairs and watched Parker pound the locks.

When at last the box was opened it was only half full, lined with neatly wrapped stacks of bills. Parker stuck a hand in among them, messing up the stacks and said, "The singles and fives are all new. We'll have to leave them."

Weiss said, "You got more good news? It wouldn't be Confederate money, would it?"

"It won't add up to much," Parker told him.

"You know what kind of day this is?" Weiss said. "I'll tell you what kind of day this is. The kind of day this is, we'll come down off this hill a couple days from now, the government will have devalued the dollar. How much is singles and fives?"

"Maybe a thousand," Parker said.

"Another two hundred fifty dollars bye-bye," Weiss said, and Uhl shot him in the head.

Four

Parker dove through the window elbows first, the rotted wood and shards of glass spraying out in front of him. He ducked his head, landed hard on his right shoulder, rolled over twice, and was running before he was well on his feet. He heard shots behind him but didn't know if they were coming at him or not. He ran for the corner of the barn, and as he went around it a bullet chunked into the wood beside his head, spitting splinters at his cheek.

He hit the dirt, rolled some more, and wound up against the side of the barn and out of sight of the house. He reached inside his coat, and his hand closed on an empty holster.

Where was it? There were no more shots from the house. Parker stood there a few seconds more, his hand still touching the empty holster, and then he moved up to the edge of the barn and cautiously looked around.

A bullet whistling by made him duck back again, but not before he saw his revolver lying in plain view in the dirt outside the window. It had come out when he'd landed.

Uhl hadn't seen it yet — he'd had too much else to think about so far — but he would. And when he did he'd come out of that house and hunt Parker down.

Andrews must be dead. And Weiss was definitely dead.

Parker moved away from the corner of the barn. If he could get inside this structure, get into one of the cars, be ready to run Uhl down with it when Uhl came in, there'd be a chance. But the only window on his side was high up in the wall, too high to reach. The only ground-floor openings into the barn were on the two sides Uhl could see from the house.

It was no good. He couldn't fight Uhl. With all this open ground around the barn and house he couldn't sneak up on Uhl.

The only thing left to do was get away from here.

On this side of the house the land fell away again into woods. There was maybe forty yards of open ground, and then the trees. Heavy woods covered the entire valley on this side.

"Parker! You left your gun behind!"

Parker moved away from the barn. He began to run down the hill.

"Parker! Come back for your gun!"

Parker bent low, and just before he reached the trees shooting started behind him. He heard the bullets snicking and scratching through the leaves over his head; like most people, Uhl was aiming too high when firing downhill.

It was cooler, damper, dimmer in under the trees. Almost like the smell and feel of the air inside the barn. There were a lot of bushes, but it was possible to work your way through. The bushes made him hard to see, and the tree trunks made him hard to hit.

He veered to the right as he went on. The shooting had stopped again, and after a minute he stopped too. He listened and heard nothing.

Would Uhl come down here to get him? It would almost even the odds, the two of them in the woods. He might get behind Uhl, he might get the edge on him. Or he might even get out of the woods with Uhl still in them, get back up the slope to the house, get one of the other guns in there. If Uhl wasn't carrying all four guns with him.

Parker moved again. He still could hear nothing from Uhl. He headed back at a sharp angle so he'd come out far to the right of where he'd gone in. He wanted to know what Uhl was up to. He had to know what Uhl was up to. Could he afford to leave Parker alive, could he take a chance on that? Or would he think it a bigger chance to come in here after Parker? Which chance would he want to take?

Ahead, through the trees, Parker could see the grassy slope. He moved more cautiously, bent forward, his suit and shoes the wrong clothing for this place and this kind of stalking. But he needed to leave the suit jacket on — the white shirt would be too obvious a target. And black street oxfords were still better than no shoes at all.

He heard the car start. He went forward to the edge of the woods, looking up, and saw Uhl back his Chevy out of the barn. He left the motor running and hurried into the house, and a minute later he came out with two small cardboard suitcases. They'd had four of those, one for each of them to carry his share away in, but it had apparently taken only two to transport the entire haul.

Uhl put the two cases in the trunk of the Chevy and then came by the side of the barn to look downslope at the woods. He didn't see Parker, and Parker couldn't make out the expression on his face. After a minute he turned and went back into the house.

Go up the slope? Try to get to the car? It looked too much like a trap, left out there running with the money in it. Parker waited.

Uhl came running back out. Why running? He suddenly seemed to be feeling much more urgency than before. He ran around the Chevy and into the barn.

What was he up to? Parker's hands were closed into his fists, but there was nothing he could do; he could only stand and watch and wait to see what Uhl did next.

Smoke. Curling out the broken windows of the house.

The son of a bitch had set the house on fire.

Parker moved out of the woods and ran crouching to the right until the barn was between him and the house, and then he ran up the hill. He knew what Uhl was up to in the barn, and if he could get there before Uhl was set, there was still a chance.

He couldn't. He heard the roar of Uhl's car before he got up as far as the barn, and as he came running around the barn he saw the Chevy bumping and slewing down the farther slope toward the dirt road.

The house was really burning now, the old wood catching fast and burning hot. Flames stuck their tongues out all the empty

22

windows. He could feel the heat on his face.

The barn. He turned toward the entrance to the barn, and when the car in there blew up it knocked him flat.

Five

Nighttime. Parker sat in darkness, his back against a tree. It was cold now, and even damper in the woods than it had been in daytime.

The fire was long since out, but there was still light on top of the hill. Arc lights had been set up around the perimeter of the hilltop, all pointed inward, glaring their harsh, shadowless light on the burnt-out wreckage like the illumination of the infield during a night game. In that glare men moved back and forth like actors in the movie, and it was impossible to believe there were any rational reasons for all that activity up there. It was as though a director somewhere had told them to mill around, and that's what they were doing, but none of them knew why.

It had been a long wait down here, and it wasn't over yet. When the Mercury had blown up it had spread the fire to the grass all around, and when Parker had come out of a semi-daze and staggered back to his feet it was to find both the barn and house sheets of flame and the whole hilltop running orange. He'd been standing on bare ground in the middle of it all, the heat evaporating the sweat off his face.

He'd come leaping and jumping through the flames and down the slope into the woods again, knowing some sort of fire department would have to respond to this sooner or later before it got downslope and set the whole woods ablaze. A man dressed in a suit and white shirt and tie, carrying identification that could quickly be proved phony, should not be found here with the burned bodies of two murdered men and one blown-up car — not half an hour after a robbery in a town twelve miles away. Parker worked his way deep into the woods, the ground sloping gradually downward, till he came to a small, quick, cold, shallow stream that ran down the bottom line of the valley. He went across that and a little ways farther, and when he found a dry grassy spot he sat down to wait.

He heard the sirens when the fire engines arrived, but he was too far away to see them or see how much work they had to do. He waited, listening, hearing nothing more, and by early afternoon he was hungry. Were there any edible berries in season now? He didn't know. He'd been born and raised in cities; these woods were another world.

When his watch said three o'clock he got up and stretched and moved again. He drank some water at the stream, washed his face, and moved on. He came to the edge of the woods and looked up, and both house and barn were gone; nothing left but a few blackened sticks jutting up. The grass was charred and black halfway down the slope.

The fire engines were gone too, but they had been replaced. The hilltop was full of police cars, and as Parker watched, a white closed van arrived with blue lettering on the sides: MOBILE LAB.

So it was going to be a wait. But he wasn't likely to get anywhere striking off blindly into those woods behind him. It was the road or nothing, and until the law finished up there it was going to be nothing.

But it was taking them a while. They swarmed over the hill like ants. Cars came and went, trucks arrived, men roamed back and forth, and at one point toward twilight a roaring, fluttering helicopter even dangled down out of the sky and visited for a few minutes before being reeled up and away again like a noisy fishing lure.

In a way, the length of time they were taking up there irritated Parker, because they were delaying him and causing him trouble; but in another way it pleased him, because it meant Uhl and the money were still at large. They were hunting here for something to tell them where to look next, and Parker knew they wouldn't find a thing.

Parker usually could be patient, but this was the worst kind of waiting. He was cold and stiff, the air was damp, he hadn't eaten since this morning before the robbery plus one can of beer after, and he had no way of knowing how much longer the wait would last. It was now past midnight, and they were still there.

From time to time he moved around at the edge of the woods only to keep limber and help the circulation. He was moving now, when light suddenly flashed past the trees all around him, and he dropped at once to the ground and lay there not moving.

The flash wasn't repeated. He waited and nothing more happened, and finally he raised himself up behind a tree and looked up the slope and saw that the arc lights were being taken down and stored in a truck. One of them, being moved while still lit, had happened to be pointed in his direction for a second; that's all it had been.

It took them ten minutes more, but finally there were no lights left but the headlights of a few cars and trucks, and then those swung away and disappeared down the farther slope and there was darkness.

Parker cautiously came up the slope. The night was clear, with a quarter moon giving silver-blue light, enough so he could make out shapes in the darkness. Parker made it to the top, saw nothing but beaten-down emptiness and burned-down husks, and moved on.

There was no point looking for the thin track up here. He went wading down through thick dew-wet grass until he came to the dirt road and then turned left. He walked half a mile to the highway and turned left again. He didn't like going back to the town where they'd knocked over the bank, but it was the only one close enough to walk to.

He saw headlights far away and got off the road and crouched behind bushes in a field. The car went by, red taillights receding, and then he got up and moved on again. Far away he could see the pale dome of light in the sky where the town was.

Six

Parker let the police car go by and then stepped out of the doorway and moved on around the corner. It was after midnight — cars on the streets were few, all the bars were shut, there was no one out walking.

In the center of town there would still be some activity. The bus depot would be open, and an all-night diner. There would be plenty of action around police headquarters. But Parker was staying away from all that. He was a stranger in town; he had thirty-seven dollars in his pockets; he carried identification claiming he was Thomas Lynch from Newark, New Jersey, but one phone call would expose that as false. He wasn't about to show himself if he could help it.

A block away he could see a gas station, shut for the night. He'd tried two already, but neither had been any good, and the longer he walked around this town the more risk he ran. He moved quickly toward the corner.

There were two cars parked against the fence beside the station building. That was a hopeful sign, maybe. He went over to them and checked, but neither had the keys in the ignition. He could jump the wires, but that way was messy and complicated if he had to stop for gas or something to eat. He'd prefer keys if he could get them. One of the cars, the old Ford, had a jack handle on the floor in back. Parker took that and went over to the station building. The main office door was all one sheet of glass, so he went to the overhead garage door, which was smaller panes of glass, broke one pane, and reached through to unlock the door. He slid it up, stepped inside, and shut the door again.

The cash register was empty as he'd assumed it would be. On a pegboard on the side wall were hung two sets of keys. The first included a Ford key, so he put it back. The other included a

Chrysler company key, and the second car parked outside was a Dodge Polara, about a year old.

Parker took the Dodge key and left the others on the chain. He went out the way he'd come in, got into the Dodge, and started the engine. It turned over right away. He had no idea what sort of work it had been left here for or if the work had been done, but the engine ran and that was all that mattered. He backed out in a tight U-turn, drove out to the street, and three minutes later was out on the highway again, headed out of town.

Twenty miles away there was an interstate road. Parker made it in sixteen minutes, seeing no traffic along the way, and went up the ramp and headed east. He drove seven hours with one side trip for gas. He crossed two state lines, and when he was over five hundred miles from the town where the hit had taken place he took an exit ramp and a blacktop road, and as the sun was coming up in his eyes he drove into a good-sized city. He left the car on a side street in a residential section and took a local bus. It carried him downtown with a lot of working people. He got off, asked directions to the railroad station, and walked there. He checked the schedules and found there was a train leaving for Cleveland at ten past nine, not quite two hours from now. He bought a ticket and then went and had breakfast, and then he had nine dollars left.

He slept on the train. Going through the station in Cleveland he picked up a suitcase that was standing there. He walked to a hotel and checked in as Thomas Lynch, saying he would be staying three days. He went up to his room and slept again and came down that evening to send a wire to his woman, Claire, in New Orleans:

DELAY. WIRE 5 C c/o ALDERBAN HOTEL, TOM LYNCH

Then he went and had dinner. Afterwards he went upstairs to his room again and looked in the suitcase. He'd picked it up just to have luggage for the sake of the desk clerk, but on the other hand it would be nice to know what was in it. It wasn't locked.

28

He put it on the bed and opened it.

Two suits, a dark gray and a medium brown, both meant for a short and very wide man who still believed in eighteen-inch cuffs. Three white shirts with wide collars and French cuffs. Four ties, all with diagonal stripes and muted colors. Boxer shorts. Undershirts. Black socks and dark green socks. Three sets of cuff links, one with Roman emperors, one with rabbit silhouettes, one with horses' heads, and three matching tie clasps. A deck of cards with pornographic pictures on the back in red and blue. Various Jade East toiletries. A toothbrush and toothpaste for sensitive gums. Electric razor. A packet of business cards:

JOHN "JACK" HORGAN
CATBIRD PLUMBING SUPPLIES CORP.
St. Louis, Mo.
You're Sitting On the Catbird Seat

A pint of Ballantine Scotch. An address book full of business firms. Bottles of aspirin and Alka-Seltzer, and a tube of unidentified prescription ointment.

Parker put everything back except the scotch and stowed the suitcase in the closet. Then he watched television awhile before going back to sleep.

Late the next morning he picked up his five hundred at the Western Union office in the lobby. He went out of the hotel and walked four blocks to an antique store in a run-down side street. The inside of the place was packed and crammed and dusty. It looked to be mostly junk, antique only in the sense that it was old.

An old bell had rung the door when he'd pushed it open and after a minute a very thin, straight old woman came out of the back somewhere. She had gray hair tightly gathered in a bun at the back of her head, her dress was black and dusty, and her bifocals had thin metal frames and round lenses. Her lips were thin. She said, "May I be of service?" Briskly, not caring much.

Parker looked at her. "I wanted to talk to Dempsey," he said.
"Mr. Dempsey passed on," she said. "I'm in charge now."
Parker was doubtful. He said, "I'm interested in guns."
"Antique guns?"
"Sure."
"Well, we do have some," she said. She seemed somewhat doubtful herself now. "Some very nice old derringers, for instance."
"I had something a little different in mind," Parker said.
She looked at him through the lower part of the bifocals, then the upper part again. "Were you a customer of Mr. Dempsey's?"
"I was recommended by a customer of his," Parker said.
"Who would that be?"
"Fellow named Grofield."
"Oh, the actor." She smiled. "Yes, I remember Mr. Grofield. A charming young man."
Parker didn't care about that. He said, "He's the one told me about Dempsey."
"Of course," she said. "Then you'll want to see some of our special stock, won't you?"
"That's right."
"Come along," she said.
He went with her down the narrow aisle between the seatless chairs, the craked vases, the chipped enamel basins, the scarred chifferobes. Everywhere there was frayed cloth, cracked leather, sagging upholstery, chipped veneer, and an overall aura of dust and disuse and tired old age.

The doorway at the back was low enough so Parker had to duck his head. The old woman led him through a narrow kitchen containing equipment almost as old and tired-looking as the wares in the shop, and then through another low door and down a flight of stairs into a low-ceilinged basement full of more ancient furniture. It was impossible to see how half of it had been maneuvered down the narrow stairs, or why anyone had bothered.

The old woman said, "What do you need?"

"Handguns. Two of them. Alike, if possible."

"Well, let's see. You wait here."

He waited. She went away and disappeared into the dimness around a Victorian loveseat with a medallion back. Parker waited, occasionally hearing a small sound from the general area ahead of him, and then she came back carrying two shoeboxes. She set these down on a handy dusty surface and opened them up. "Both alike," she said.

They were two Smith & Wesson Terriers, a five-shot .32 revolver with a two-inch barrel. A good gun for carrying unobtrusively, good in close quarters, but no good at any range at all and not packing a very hard wallop.

Parker said, "Nothing heavier than that?"

"Not two alike," she said.

He picked up the guns and hefted them. They were both empty. They both looked in good shape, with their front sights, with no obvious scratches or dents. Parker clicked the triggers of both and said, "How much?"

She thought it over, frowning at the guns in his hands. Then, very doubtfully, she said, "A hundred for the two?" As though sure he'd argue with her. And before he could say anything she added hastily, "And a box of shells you get too."

"That's all right," Parker said.

"It is?" She didn't believe he wasn't going to haggle with her.

"A hundred for the two," he said. He put the guns back in their shoeboxes and reached for his wallet.

"That's fine, then," she said. "I'll go get the shells."

She went away and got the shells, and when she came back Parker had two fifties in his hand. She handed him the shells, and he handed her the money. She thanked him and said, "You know, I'd rather you didn't load them in the store here."

"I wasn't going to."

"That's fine. Shall I put some string around the boxes?"

"Yeah, do that."

She put the lids on the boxes and started to carry them away, but Parker said, "Bring the string here, why don't you?"

She looked surprised. "Oh, I see! Of course." She went away, came back with a roll of twine, and said, "I wouldn't give you empty boxes. Sooner or later you'd just find out and come back. And where else do I have to go but here?" She tied the two boxes together while she talked. "That's the one kind of person you can trust," she said. "The person who doesn't have anyplace else to go."

Parker didn't say anything to that.

When the package was tied, the woman led the way back upstairs, Parker following with the shoeboxes under his arm.

Upstairs, Parker said, "You know where I can buy a car in this town?"

She nodded at the shoeboxes. "That way, you mean?"

"Where I won't be asked questions," Parker said.

"That's what I meant," she said. "Yes, there's a very good place I know. It's not very far from here."

"Would you call them and tell them I'm on the way over?"

"Certainly."

He waited while she made the call, and then she went outside with him and gave him the directions. It was another sunny day, and she looked out of place out here in the brightness with the dust and the age still on her. As though she were left over from some prior world.

Parker walked to the place she'd told him about, a used-car lot in a nightbourhood of used-car lots. It took some dickering because what he wanted was a mace, a car with papers that looked good and plates that looked good, but half an hour later the deal was set on a two-year-old Pontiac with standard shift and a bad tendency to pull to the left. The car had been in an accident and had rolled, but it would take him where he wanted to go and it wasn't on anybody's list of hot cars and the plates would also be clean and cool, and that was all that mattered.

The dealer drove him to a Western Union office where he wired Claire for more money. He got it forty-five minutes later, went back to the lot, traded the cash for the car, and drove out of the lot. He stopped in several downtown stores and bought a suitcase and gradually filled it with clothing and toilet articles. He didn't bother to go back to the hotel because there was nothing there but a suitcase he didn't own, and there was no point making a special trip to pay the bill. When he was done with his shopping he drove south out of Cleveland, and when he was near the entrance to the Ohio Turnpike he pulled off the road, opened the package of shoeboxes, took out the guns, threw the shoeboxes out the window, and loaded the guns. Then he got out of the car and walked a little ways into the woods beside the road and fired each gun twice into a nearby tree. They both worked all right. He reloaded, put the guns away in his pockets, and went back to the car.

Now to find Uhl.

TWO

One

Parker sat in the darkness in the hotel room and waited for the phone to ring. He had questions, and all he could do now was sit around and wait for the answers.

He heard the shuffling of slippers along the walk out front and knew it was Madge coming to talk to him. That was the only thing wrong with her, the only thing wrong with this place of hers — she liked to talk too much. But it was safe; he could stay here and make his phone calls from here, so he was willing to put up with a little inconvenience.

He hoped the fact that the room was in darkness would keep her away, but he didn't really expect anything to save him, and he wasn't surprised when she rapped sharply on the door.

"Parker! Turn on some lights and open up! What's the matter with you?"

Parker got up and switched on a table lamp and went over to open the door. He said, "Don't yell my name all over the country."

Madge came in saying, "Brother, you're almost the only client I got. I don't know what's the matter with kids these days. I brought ice." She held up the plastic bucket. "You got anything to drink?"

"I've got a bottle," Parker said, and went over to the dresser to get it.

Madge dropped into a chair and let her arms dangle. "I'm gettin' old," she said.

It was true, and it had been true for a long time now. Madge was in her middle sixties now and a rarity: a hooker who'd saved her money during the good years. She'd bought this place a dozen years ago, this Green Glen Motel on Route 6 north of Scranton, and ran it herself with the assistance of a retarded young heifer named Ethel, who might or might not be Madge's daughter. The motel returned Madge a modest profit, and in a way it kept her in touch with her original profession, since most of the rooms here tended to get rented by the hour.

Because she knew a lot of the right people and because she could be trusted, Madge's place was occasionally a meeting ground for groups of men like Parker setting up an operation somewhere and was less often used as a temporary hideout by somebody on the run. Madge didn't like to risk what she had that way, but if it was an emergency she wouldn't turn a man away.

She was medium height and thin as an antenna, with sharp elbows and a shriveled throat. Her hair was white and coarse and cut very short in the Italian style worn by women forty years her junior. She was wearing dark green stretch pants tonight and a sleeveless high-neck top of green and white and amber stripes and green slip-on shoes. Great golden hoop earrings hung from her ears. She kept her eyebrows plucked and redrawn in sardonic curving lines. Her fingernails were always long and curved and covered in blood-red polish, but she wore no lipstick, so that her mouth was one more thin pale line in a heavily lined face.

If she'd had less toughness and assurance, the effect would have been pretty bad, particularly with the gleaming white false teeth she flashed every time she opened her mouth, but somehow or other she had the style to get away with it. The young clothes weren't being worn by an old body but by a young spirit. In some incomprehensible way, Madge had stopped getting older along about 1920.

Parker had come here because he'd needed a base for a little while and he'd known Madge was safe. He could make his phone calls without anybody listening in. He could stay here as long as he wanted without anybody ever getting curious about who he was or where he came from or what he was all about. For all of that, listening to Madge talk was a small price to pay.

As he brought her a drink now she said, "An old friend of

yours was here a while ago. Smiles Kastor."

Parker nodded. "I remember Kastor," he said.

"He's doing okay for himself," she said. She swallowed some whiskey and launched into nostalgia.

Parker didn't really listen at all. He sat across from her, an untasted drink in his hand, and at intervals he nodded or made some small comment. That was all she needed, just an indication every once in a while that she still had her audience.

What he was mostly doing, sitting there, was waiting for the phone to ring. He had three calls out, and there was nothing to do right now but wait.

Madge talked on for an hour and said something interesting only once, and that was when she sat up and snapped her fingers and said, "You know, I forgot all about it. I bet you did too. I have some money of yours."

"You do?"

"You and Handy McKay came through here about four years ago; you had some jewelry you wanted unloaded."

"That's right," Parker said. "I forgot about that."

"Your share's twenty-two hundred," she said. "I have it in the safe out in the office. You want it?"

"Hold on to it," he said. "Take my bill out of it when I leave."

"Okay, fine," she said.

It was good to have stashes in safe places here and there around the country. You never knew when you might need it. A Claire wasn't always available, sitting on your case money a telegram away.

But it was stupid to have forgotten the money here. Parker remembered how that had happened; the jewelry had been an afterthought, an unexpected side result of him and Handy going up to Buffalo after a man named Bronson, a wheel in a gambling syndicate that called itself the Outfit. Bronson had put a contract out on Parker because of some trouble there'd been, and Parker made some more trouble, and Bronson's successor decided to let the contract lapse. In all of that, the handful of jewelry Handy had found in Bronson's safe got itself forgotten.

But this is where they'd come after they'd finished with Bronson, and they'd given Madge the jewelry to unload for them, and here she was four years later with twenty-two hundred bucks out of nowhere.

She said, "What about Handy? Think I should send it to him?"

"He's supposed to call me in a little while. I'll ask him."

"He retired, didn't he?"

"Yes."

She waited and then said, "Say something, Parker. God, to get you to gossip it's like pulling teeth."

"Handy retired," Parker said.

"I *know* he retired! Tell me about it. Tell me why he retired, tell me where he is, how's he doing. Talk to me, Parker, Goddammit."

So Parker talked to her, telling her about Handy, running a diner now up in Presque Isle, Maine. She listened for a while, but she could never go very long without doing her own talking, so soon enough she interrupted him to tell him about somebody else she knew who'd retired seven different times in a space of twenty years, and Parker went back to his own silence again, not listening, waiting for the phone.

It rang half an hour later. Madge said, "You want me to leave?"

"It don't matter, stick around." He went over and picked up the phone and said hello.

Madge said, "Is it Handy?"

It wasn't. Parker shook his head at her and said into the phone, "How'd we do?"

"Bad. A couple of guys heard of Uhl, but I couldn't find anybody who worked with him or knew how to get in touch with him. Matt Rosenstein drew a fat blank. Listen, I don't know what you want these two for, but if it's work a couple of other boys are interested."

"It's a special situation," Parker said.

"Well, I'm sorry I couldn't help you out."

40

"That's okay." Parker hung up and went back and sat down. Madge said, "You looking for information?"

"Yes."

"I'm the girl to ask, Parker. Try me."

"George Uhl."

Her expectant look faded slowly. "Uhl? George Uhl? He must be new."

"Pretty new. He's worked six times, he said. He said one time he worked with Matt Rosenstein. The way he said it, Rosenstein should be hot stuff, but I never heard of him."

"No, you wouldn't," she said. "Matt Rosenstein, I know him. You wouldn't ever cross his path. You two have different kinds of outlooks."

"Tell me about him," Parker said.

"He's a scavenger bird," she said. "He pulls things nobody else wants. He's done a couple of kidnappings, he was a whiskey hijacker along the Canadian border for a while, he's been all over."

"He doesn't do the big hits?"

"Oh, them too," she said. "With a pretty respectable string sometimes, too. He'll work any racket he comes across, so a few times it's been your sort of thing. But he's too wild; a lot of smart ones won't work with him. I've heard it said he's a snowbird, but I don't think he's on anything. He's just one of those naturally wild ones. If this George Uhl thinks Matt Rosenstein is hot stuff, it tells you a lot about George Uhl. Like you probably shouldn't work with him."

"Too late to tell me that," Parker said. "He came recommended by Benny Weiss."

"Benny's okay," she said and shrugged. "But anybody can make a mistake."

"Where do I find Rosenstein, do you know?"

She shook her head. "I'm sorry, I don't. I know who he is. He's been here once or twice with a bunch, but I wouldn't know how to reach him or even who would know how."

"That's what —"

The phone sounded again. Parker broke off what he was saying and went over to answer it, and this time it was Handy McKay. He nodded at Madge and said to Handy, "Get anywhere?"

"Not on Uhl. He's too new, I guess. But I found out about Matt Rosenstein."

"Where he is?"

"He's like you," Handy said. "You don't contact him direct. Just like people with a message for you come to me, people with a message for Rosenstein go to somebody else."

"Who?"

"A guy named Brock, in New York. Paul Brock. He runs a record store there."

"Hold on while I get a pencil."

Madge was already on her feet. "I'll get it."

She got him pencil and paper, and Parker put down Brock's name and address. Madge whispered, "Tell him about the money," and Parker nodded.

Handy said, "That's all I could get."

"That's fine," Parker said. "Madge says she's got twenty-two hundred bucks belongs to you. Remember those jewels we took away from Bronson that time?"

"Christ, yes! I forget about that."

"She wants to know should she send you the money or hold it for you."

"Send it."

Parker was surprised. "You don't want it stashed?"

"What do I want it stashed for? I'm not going anyplace. I run a diner now, Parker. That's what I do."

"Okay," Parker said. "I'll tell her. And thanks for the stuff on Rosenstein."

"Any time."

Parker hung up and told Madge she was to send the money and gave her Handy's address. Then the phone rang again and it was the third man Parker had called, and he had the Brock name too but nothing else. Parker thanked him for it and hung up and said to Madge, "I'll be going in the morning."

"You're after this boy Uhl," she said.

"Have Ethel call me at eight," Parker said.

"You always were gabby," she said, and emptied her glass. She got to her feet. "That's always been your big failing, Parker," she said. "You talk too much."

Parker locked the door after her and switched off the light. In the morning he left for New York.

Two

With enough volume to drown out a sonic boom, the loudspeaker over the doorway blared out the voices of a rock quartet declaiming the end of civilization as we know it. Album jackets hung turning from wires in the tall, narrow window beside the entrance. Rain streaked the window, further distorting the distorted photographs on the jackets.

Parker had left the car around the corner on Sixth Avenue. Discodelia, Brock's record shop, was on Blecker Street in Greenwich Village on one of the tourist blocks. Parker walked up the block in the rain and he was the only one on the sidewalk. It was late morning, too early for tourists, and a weekday. And it was raining.

He turned and went in through the open doorway under the yowling speaker. Because the sound was aimed outward, away from the shop, it was quieter inside, almost cosy.

It was a long, narrow room with a yellow floor and ceiling. A high counter and a cash register and a glum male cashier were just to the left of the entrance, and beyond that both side walls were lined with record bins. The rear wall was a montage of posters, newspaper clippings, publicity photos, and pages from old comic books. More album jackets filled the upper half of both side walls above the record bins. More records were stored underneath the bins. Three boys of about twenty were scattered through the store, flipping through the records in the bins.

Parker said to the cashier, "I'm looking for Paul Brock."

He shook his head. "He ain't in in the mornings. Try again around two, two thirty."

"I'm in a hurry," Parker said. "I'll try him at home."

"Okay," the cashier said.

Parker stood there looking at him.

The cashier frowned, not understanding. "What's the matter?"

"His address."

"Who? Paul's?"

"Naturally."

"I can't give out Paul's home address. I thought you knew it."

"If I knew it," Parker said, "I wouldn't be asking you."

"Well, I can't give it out," the cashier said. "He'd fire me, I start giving out his home address to everybody off the street."

"You know his phone number?"

The cashier shook his head. "I can't give you that either. You better come back around two, two thirty."

"I didn't ask for it, I asked do you know it."

"Sure, I know it."

"Call him."

The cashier wasn't getting it, and that was making him mad. "What the hell for?" he said.

"Ask him should you tell me his home address. Tell him there's a guy here wants to talk to him about Matt."

"The hell with that," the cashier said. "I got work to do here. You come back this afternoon."

"Don't mess around when there's things you don't understand," Parker told him.

"What's that supposed to mean?"

"Maybe Brock won't be happy that you wasted my time. Maybe you ought to find out."

The cashier hesitated. Parker knew if Paul Brock was Matt Rosenstein's go-between it was likely Brock was himself into a few things here and there, and an employee on close enough terms to speak of him by his first name would have to know at least that there were things happening under the surface of Brock's life, whether he knew exactly what they were or not. So although the feeling of urgency here was all on Parker's side, the cashier couldn't be sure of that, and he was going to have to cover himself just in case Parker *was* somebody important.

But the cashier's back was up, and he was resisting. He frowned, and hesitated, and looked past Parker at his three maybe-customers as though hoping one of them would interrupt them by buying something, and in general he let the seconds tick by without doing anything. Parker looked at his watch finally and said, "I don't have a lot of time."

"I'll see what he has to say," the cashier said sullenly and pulled a telephone out from under the counter. He was sitting on a stool and he dialed the phone in his lap, protecting it jealously so Parker wouldn't be able to see what the number was. Parker didn't bother to watch.

The cashier held the receiver to his ear a long time with nothing happening, and Parker had about decided Brock wasn't home and he was going to have to come back here this afternoon after all when the cashier suddenly said, "Paul? Artie. Listen, Paul. There's a guy here. He came in lookin' for you. He wants me to give him your address." He listened and said, "I don't know, I never saw him before." He sounded aggrieved, as though it was Parker's fault they hadn't met before. Then he listened again and said, "All I know is what I told you."

Parker reached across the counter and closed his thumb and first finger on the cashier's nose. "Don't tell fibs," he said, and squeezed, and let go.

"Ow!" Eyes watering, the cashier jumped to his feet, the stool clattering over behind him. He still kept the phone to his face, but he looked as though he'd forgotten about it. Putting his other hand over his nose, cupping the nose protectively, he said, "What are you doing? You crazy?"

"I told you it was about Matt," Parker reminded him. "Tell Brock I want to talk to him about Matt."

"Hold on, Paul," the cashier said and put the receiver down on the counter. He put both hands to his face and squinted past his bunched fingers at Parker. "That hurt, goddammit," he said. "Hey!"

Parker had picked up the receiver. The cashier lunged for it, but Parker grabbed his wrist and held. He said into the receiver,

"Brock?"

A thin voice said, "Hello? Artie? What the hell's going on there?"

"I want to talk to you about Matt," Parker said.

There was a little silence, and then the thin voice said, "Who's this? Where's Artie?"

"I'm the one wants to talk to you about Matt," Parker told him. "I'm in a hurry, and I figured you wouldn't want me talking in public here, so I thought I'd come by and talk to you at home."

"About what? Who the hell are you, for the love of God?"

"About Matt," Parker said.

"Matt? Matt who?"

"Matt Rose. You want more identification? A longer name, for instance?"

There was another silence, and then, in a quieter voice, Brock said, "No, I get you. You want to talk about him, huh?"

"That's right."

"You got a message for him?"

"I want to talk about him."

"Christ, you're a one-track mind. You want to talk about him, you want to talk about him, you want to talk about him. What did you do to my cashier?"

Parker was still holding the cashier's wrist. He'd tried to get away a couple of times, but each time Parker had bent his arm for him, so now he just stood there, breathing hard, glowering at Parker, making no trouble. None of the three browsers had so much as looked up when the stool had gone over; they were all absorbed in their quests.

Parker said, "He's all right. He's right here. You want to talk to him?"

"What for? And what do I want to talk to you for?"

"I'm not trouble for you. All I want is to talk about—"

"Yeah, I know, you want to talk about Matt. Okay, okay. You know where Downing Street is?"

"I can find it."

"It's the next block down on Sixth, west side of the street. I'm in number eight, near the corner. Second floor."

"I'll leave now. You want to talk to your boy?"

"No. I'll see you."

Parker let go the cashier's hand and gave him the phone. "He doesn't want to talk to you," he said.

The cashier put the receiver to his head anyway and said, "Paul?" But Brock had already hung up, so now the cashier looked needlessly foolish and he knew it. He hung up the phone with an angry gesture, put it away under the counter, and said, "You didn't have to get tough."

"I didn't," Parker told him.

Three

"You sound like your voice. Come in."

Parker walked into a decorating magazine's idea of the perfect masculine den. Wood was everywhere, massive and darkly stained. Knurled posts, heavy rough-finished tables, lamps with deep-grained wooden bases. And leather, and black iron, and a few discreet touches of brass. The wall-to-wall carpet was vaguely Persian, with an intricate swirling design in tans and creams and dull orange against a background of black. The windows sported wood-grain shutters. Even the air-conditioner in the wall beneath the window had a wood veneer face. And through an arched open doorway done in purposely rough plaster Parker could see another room done in exactly the same style and dominated by a heavy wooden trestle table and high-backed wooden chairs with leather seats.

The outside of the building hadn't led him to expect anything like this. It was four stories high, narrow, hemmed in by similar buildings on both sides, each building having three windows facing the street on each floor and a high stoop up to a fairly ornate entrance-way. They were old buildings, old enough so that even their facelift false fronts were old — the one on this building was fake red brick - and a hallway inside had continued the same sort of first impression. Long, creaking staircases with rubber treads, bare peach-colored walls.

Paul Brock had not merely moved into the second-story floor-through apartment in this building, he'd moved an entirely different world into it. He'd put a hell of a lot of money into the place where he lived without much chance of ever getting a return on his investment, and it was a safe bet he hadn't done it all on the kind of income he was getting from that hole-in-the-wall record store. Brock was a man with other

49

things going for him, that much was sure.

Parker turned from his scanning of the apartment to study its tenant instead. The room distracted one from the man who lived in it, made him tend to disappear into the background, and maybe that was a part of the intention.

Because Paul Brock wasn't very much. Slightly under medium height, very thin, he had a long, bony neck and an Ichabod Crane sort of face, except that there was a well-worn expression of friendliness and amiability on this face. Brock wore heavy hornrimmed glasses that made his eyes look huge and his cheeks look as though they sagged. He was about thirty. He was wearing loafers and grey slacks and a pale blue short-sleeved polo shirt, and he looked like the kind of guy in the office who'd go around with a cigar box to take up the gift collection every time one of the secretaries was quitting to get married.

He shut the door now and said, "Do you have a name you give out, or do I just clear my throat when I want to attract your attention?"

"Parker."

"Parker. Nosy or pen? Ha! Well, that wasn't very funny. It's too early to offer a drink, but I—It *is* too early to offer a drink, isn't it?"

"Yes," Parker said.

"I thought it was. Coffee?"

"I don't have the time," Parker said.

"Then let's get down to business, Mr. Parker. Have a seat."

Parker sat in a wooden-armed chair with an orange seat-cushion, and Brock settled opposite him on the black leather sofa. Brock tucked his legs under himself like a woman, but it seemed an unselfconscious gesture, and in no other way did he behave overtly like a faggot. The position was somehow more childlike than sexual.

Parker leaned forward and put his elbows on knees. "First of all," he said, "I'm in the same business as Matt Rosenstein. He doesn't know me, but we've got some mutual acquaintances also in the profession. If you want, I can give you some names till we

50

come to one you know, and then you can check me out to see if I'm what I say I am."

"I have no doubt you're what you say you are," Brock said. "You couldn't be anything else. In fact, you remind me of Matt in a lot of ways. Not in appearance so much, and probably with more personal control, but still you two are obviously both in the same bag. I don't have to check on you."

"Good. There's another guy also in the same business, and I know he worked with Rosenstein once. I want to find this guy, and I don't have any way to get in touch with him. Maybe Rosenstein does. That means I have to ask Rosenstein. I asked around and I found out that if I want any answers from Rosenstein I have to ask the questions of you."

Brock nodded. "That's true," he said. "I am Matt's post office. Who is the man you want to find?"

"George Uhl," Parker said. "U-h-l." He watched Brock's face and saw nothing happen there.

"I wouldn't know him," Brock said, "but then I don't know all of Matt's friends. Why do you want to find him?"

"Business reasons," Parker said.

"None of mine, eh?" Brock smiled amiably. "That's fair enough. So what you want me to do is ask Matt how you get in touch with this man Uhl, is that right?"

"Or send me to Rosenstein," Parker said, "and I'll ask him myself."

Brocks smile got thinner. "I don't think that would be the way to handle it. Though I see no reason not to make a phone call for you. You say this man's name is George Uhl?"

"Yes."

"Odd name," Brock said. He untucked his legs and put his feet on the floor. "I'll make the call," he said, "and then we'll wait a while before Matt calls back. You understand that."

"I'll wait."

"You're making me a nervous host," Brock said. "May I at least offer you some coffee while you wait?"

"Make the call first," Parker said.

"Naturally."

Brock slid to his feet, made a smiling half-bow to excuse himself, and left the room.

Parker sat in the chair and waited. The room forced itself on his attention much more than an ordinary room. His eyes kept traveling from detail to detail, distracting his mind.

He vaguely heard the murmur of speech from deeper within the apartment. That would be Brock on the phone. Then there was silence for a while, and then Brock came in with a silver coffee service on a silver tray with a dish of chocolate chip cookies. "The cookies are homemade," he said, putting the tray down. "I think you'll find them quite good. How do you take your coffee?"

"Black."

Brock poured. The cups were ornate, with tiny, slender curved handles and fragile saucers. The spoons were smaller than ordinary. Brock put a cookie on the saucer with the cup and passed it over to Parker.

It was like Madge again. Waiting for a phone call and spending the meantime in somebody else's idea of social fun. Coffee and cookies. Parker ate some of the cookie, and it had a good taste to it.

Brock perched on the edge of the sofa, stirring milk and sugar into his own coffee, said, "Artie phoned me back, you know. After you left the store."

"He did?"

"He said you tweaked his nose." Brock smiled merrily. "What a strange thing to do," he said.

Parker shrugged. He drank some of the coffee, and that was good, too.

Brock kept a small conversation going awhile longer, talking about Artie, about the record store, about the rain beating down outside, and Parker answered him the way he'd answered Madge, with nods and monosyllables. But the combination of small talk, hot coffee, and the distracting detail-full room were soporific. Also the vague shush of rain outside the shuttered windows. Parker sat back in the chair and let his body relax while he waited.

After a while Brock said, "Excuse me. I'll be right back." Parker nodded, and Brock left.

The room was full of details. The rain whispered outside. The coffee was warm in his stomach. His eyelids were drooping.

When he realized he'd been drugged it was too late to do anything about it. He was too weak to stand. A swirling dizziness was spinning up from his stomach, clouding his sight, befuddling his brain.

He managed to turn his head and look at the doorway to the dining room, the rough plaster arch. It was empty. The dining room beyond, heavy with wooden furniture like a room in a monastery, was empty.

The guns were heavy, his pockets confining, but he got the guns out, he got them out. He pushed forward and went to his knees onto the rug, the rug muffling the thump. He swayed forward and made it to the sofa, a revolver loosely held in each hand. He stuffed the guns under the pillows, deep in under the pillows.

Night was closing in, full of swirling mists. On hands and knees he moved his heavy dead body away from the sofa, back toward the orange chair. He wasn't making it. He lunged forward, and miles away some rocky cliff that was his forehead blundered into the wooden chair arm, and he fell, turning, and darkness wrapped a black wool blanket around him hours before he hit the floor.

Four

Floating. Floating. Blue and blue and black. Bottom of the ocean. Outer space, between the stars. Tiny winking lights millions of miles away. Soft floating, wrapped in dark blue cotton candy. Soft blankets. Endlessly turning. Slow.

"Can you hear me?"

Irritation. A rip in the fabric. But still the floating.

"Can you hear me?"

Answer. Easier that way. "Yes."

"What do you want with George Uhl?"

"Money."

"What money?"

"My money. Our money."

"George Uhl has money belonging to you? Does he?"

"Yes."

"How did he get your money?"

"Double cross."

"On a robbery?"

"Yes."

"Tell me about the robbery."

Complicated question. Irritation. Painful.

"Tell me about the robbery."

Easier to answer. "Bank. Four string. Benny Weiss. Phil Andrews. George Uhl. Thirty-three grand. Uhl shot Weiss. Shot Andrews. Burned house down."

"How did you get away?"

"Out window."

"Does he know you're still alive?"

"Yes."

"Was thirty-three thousand your piece or the whole pie?"

"Whole."

"Do you know where George Uhl is?"

"No."

"Do you know how to find him?"

"Matt Rosenstein. Ask Matt Rosenstein."

"Any other way?"

"No."

"There aren't any other links to Uhl?"

"Benny Weiss."

"Isn't he dead?"

"Yes."

"So Rosenstein is the only lead you have."

. . .

"So Rosenstein is the only lead you have."

. . .

"Is Rosenstein the only lead you have?"

"Yes."

"Do you have any other business with Rosenstein?"

"No."

"Are you a threat to Rosenstein?"

"No."

"Can you find Uhl if Rosenstein won't help you?"

Hard question. Irritation. Pain.

"Can you find Uhl if Rosenstein won't help you?"

"No. Maybe. No. Maybe some way."

"How?"

"Don't know."

"What will you do if you can't find Uhl?"

"Something else."

"That's good. Good-bye, Mr. Parker."

Floating. Blue. Blue and black. Deeper. Drowning in blue and black. Going down. Going out. Gone.

Five

His head was splitting. A violent, vicious headache driving him into consciousness. He groaned, and moved, and felt a hard, rough surface grate beneath him.

He squeezed open his eyes, and an inch away there was the jagged texture of concrete. He moved and felt the concrete against his body, and knew he was lying face down on concrete. In semidarkness, at night, with electric lighting somewhere not too close.

His head was grinding as though his brain had been cut in half and a piece of sandpaper was struck between the two halves and the halves were rubbing against it. He felt as though his skull were cracked from the top of his nose up over his forehead and across the top of his head and down to the back of his neck. The pain was so sharp it was keeping him awake and threatening to knock him out again at the same time.

He couldn't just lie here like this. He struggled until his hands were under his chest, and then he pushed upward, and shifted, and cringed against the redoubled pain in his head, and finally got himself to a sitting position.

There were black brick walls around him. Down to the right there was an open space, and beyond that a streetlight shining on a stretch of empty sidewalk and some parked cars.

What was that stink, sweet and pulpy? He grimaced away from it, his head grinding again at every movement, and then he realized the smell was on his clothes. They were damp and slightly sticky.

Sneaky Pete. Cheap port wine, wino's blood. It had been

poured over him like a baptism; he stank of dollar-a-gallon wine. His mind was confused. He remembered everything, but when he tried to think about it, put the elements together, his head would start to grind again.

Drugged, he'd been drugged, and this was the aftereffect. If only it was still raining. The water would help to soothe his head and wash the stink off his clothes. But it had stopped long enough ago so that the concrete around him was dry.

What time was it? He moved slowly to look at his watch, and it was gone. He patted his pockets and they were empty. He'd been stripped clean. He was lucky he still had his shoes.

Using the wall for support, he struggled to his feet. He threatened to pass out again for a second, but the nausea and dizziness faded grudgingly and he made it to his feet. Keeping one hand against the wall of the alley, he moved heavily and unevenly out to the street.

There was a theater marquee just to the left, dark, with a title on it in French. Past the streetlight in the other direction was an intersection and a traffic light. As he watched, the light switched to red in his direction and two cars went across the intersection from right to left.

He moved slowly down the street to the intersection, keeping close to walls for support. This was a main street here, wide and empty. He looked at the street signs and it was Sixth Avenue—Avenue of the Americas, the sign said—and he was way downtown. Even farther than Brock's record store and apartment.

Up that way was his car, but he didn't have the keys to it now. There was another set in the hotel room, but that wasn't going to do him any good till he got there.

An empty cab came up Sixth, he flagged it. It veered toward him, and then veered away again and sped by. He stepped back and leaned against a telephone pole and looked down at himself and saw that no cabdriver was going to pick him up. He looked like a bum and a drunk, he staggered, his clothes were a stained and wrinkled mess, and he looked big enough to be dangerous.

And he had no money.

He was staying at a midtown hotel. The only thing to do was to walk it, two and a half miles up Sixth Avenue. He pushed away from the telephone pole and started to walk.

A little later he passed Downing Street. Brock's apartment was just around the corner, but he was in no shape to do anything about Brock now. There'd be time for that.

It was irritating to have to walk right by his own car. He could have broken in maybe, crossed the wires, but his nerves were too unstrung for any delicate work now; his hands were shaking. And it would be stupid to have a cop come by and grab him for breaking into his own car. By the time he got done explaining the cop would just be getting interested.

There were almost no other pedestrians, very little traffic. A clock in the window of a dry cleaners he passed said four twenty-five. It was the closest thing to a dead time in New York, the bars closed and the straight people not yet out and moving.

Every once in a while as he walked a police prowl car would roll slowly by, and each time he could sense the cops in it giving him the once-over, but he just kept moving. He knew he looked and acted like a drunk, and he knew New York City cops didn't bother drunks unless they got troublesome or wandered into the wrong neighbourhood.

It took him an hour and ten minutes to get to his hotel, and then the night clerk looked at him with repugnance and disbelief.

"I was mugged and rolled," Parker said. "My room key was stolen. I need another one. The name's Lynch, room seven three three."

"One moment," the clerk said and made no secret of checking his cards to see if somebody named Lynch was really checked into room 733. Parker knew the stink of cheap wine was still rolling off him and he knew what the night clerk was thinking, but there was nothing to be done about it.

The clerk shut his little file drawer and came back to the desk. "Yes, Mr. Lynch," he said. He made no move to get a key. "You say you were robbed?"

"I say I was mugged and rolled," Parker said, "and a bottle of wine was poured on me."

"Have you reported this to the police?"

"What's the point? You ever see anybody get picked up for mugging in this town?"

The clerk made a small move toward the telephone on the desk. "Shall I phone them for you?"

"You want to make a phone call," Parker said, "you can call the house doctor."

"Did this happen on hotel premises?"

"I need rest," Parker said. "You're keeping me from rest—that's happening on the hotel premises. In the morning I'll talk to the cops, but right now I'm worn out and sick."

The clerk wasn't sure which way to go. He said, "I could have a bellboy go up to the room with you if you like." Because if Parker was legitimate it was a helpful gesture, and if he wasn't legitimate it would expose him.

"That's good," Parker said. "Bring him on."

"One moment, sir." The clerk rang his bell and turned away to get a key.

The bellboy was a short stocky elderly Negro with two gold teeth. The clerk handed him the key and said, "Would you assist Mr. Lynch to his room? He was assaulted."

"Yes, sir."

They rode up in the elevator together, and Parker said, "I was rolled. I don't have any cash on me. I'll have to take care of you tomorrow night."

"That's perfectly okay, sir."

The bellboy let him into the room, switched on the light for him, and put the key on the dresser. "Good night, sir."

"Good night."

The bellboy left, and Parker took off his shoes and got into the shower fully dressed. He let the water rinse the wine out of his suit and shirt, then stripped the wet clothes off and left them in the bottom of the tub. He showered, put a "Do Not Disturb" sign on the door, and collapsed in the bed.

59

The last thing he thought was: *It wasn't Brock's voice. Somebody else asked the questions.* But before he could study this thought his mind opened and dropped him into a valley of folded black towels and he was gone.

Six

The fourth key worked. Parker cautiously slid the door open and slipped into Brock's apartment. The living room in semidarkness looked like the entrance to a second-class Cairo hotel. Parker shut the door softly, leaned against it, listened.

No sound. No lights on anywhere that he could see. He'd gone by the record store and Brock hadn't been there, but maybe he wasn't home either.

After a minute Parker moved again, crossing the room swiftly and silently. He looked under the sofa cushions, and the guns were still there. He put one in his pocket, kept the other in his right hand, and moved on to look through the rest of the apartment.

It was empty. All the rooms continued the same wood and leather and iron and brass motif, the heavy veneer of masculinity. The kitchen was large, with a lot of chopping-block surface and with copper-bottomed pots hung on display on a pegboard on one wall. The only bedroom, dominated by a king-size bed with a maroon spread on it, had the inevitable shuttered windows plus a heavy Spanish mirror in an ornate frame and rough-textured dark dressers from Mexico. Bullfight posters gleamed dully on the walls, and the closet contained men's clothing in two different sizes.

There'd been somebody else here all along. Rosenstein? Whoever he was, it had been his voice that had done the questioning.

If only he could remember more of the specific questions that had been asked, but it was all very vague and fuzzy in his mind.

He had two general impressions: that he had been asked questions about Uhl and the robbery and the double cross, and that he had been asked questions about whether or not he was any kind of threat to Rosenstein. He couldn't really remember that much about his own answers except that he assumed he'd been truthful. He'd been given some sort of drug that relaxed the controlling part of his mind, and he had no doubt he would have told them any damn thing they wanted to know.

So they knew about Uhl and the double cross, and they knew he was looking for Uhl. The question was, what would they do with that information? Warn Uhl? Or would Rosenstein go after Uhl and the money himself?

In either case, Rosenstein had the lead on him now. Or whoever the second guy had been.

In a strange way, that cut his own feeling of urgency to nothing. Being hopelessly behind, he now knew it was impossible no matter what he did to get to Uhl first, to come at him with the advantage of surprise. So now there was no need to hurry. Now he would do things a different way.

He began by searching the apartment, making it a long and thorough job. He found his wallet and keys in a dresser drawer, and in two other locations he found two caches of money, one with four hundred dollars and the other with just under two thousand. He found two rifles in a closet and three pistols inside a round hassock. He slit open all cushions and stuffed furniture, stripped the backs of all pictures, emptied the canisters in the kitchen, looked inside the toilet in the bathroom. He ripped out suit linings, took the bed apart, emptied dresser drawers to check them for false bottoms, and then left them on the floor.

Behind the false back of the medicine chest in the bathroom he found the syringe and the small unmarked bottle. He set them aside for later.

The only thing he didn't find was any reference to the identity of the second man. There were two toothbrushes in the bathroom, two sets of clothing in the bedroom, small indications here and there throughout the apartment of the second man's presence, but nothing that gave his name, nothing to say who he was. There were old envelopes and bills addressed to Brock, there were handkerchiefs in the dresser initialled PB, but for the second man there was nothing.

And no suitcases. He thought of that later when he was done with everything, when the place was a junkyard, a Midwestern town after a twister has been through. He stood in the middle of the living room and thought things over, and then it came to him there hadn't been any suitcases.

He went back to the wreckage of the bedroom and opened the wide closet doors. Up on the shelf there were some things tucked to the side—a couple of hats and a scarf, things like that—but the middle was empty.

And the dresser drawers hadn't always been full. And there'd been a dozen or more empty hangers in the closet.

They were both gone somewhere?

Parker went back into the living room, found the phone book and the phone, looked up the number of Brock's record store, and dialed it. When someone answered, Parker said, "Hey, is Paul there? This is Bernie from Capitol Records."

"No, he isn't here now."

"Be in this afternoon?"

"He won't be in all week. He had to go away for a few days. You want me to have him call you when he gets back?"

"He'll be back the beginning of the week?"

"He wasn't sure. You want me to tell him to call you?"

"Sure. It isn't important. Tell him Bernie from Capitol Records."

"Okay."

Parker hung up and dropped the phone on the floor. Then he got to his feet and prowled around the apartment, but it had nothing else to tell him. It couldn't tell him where Brock and the other guy were now, or what they were doing. It couldn't tell him where Uhl was, and that was still the key.

He remembered part of the question-answer session from last night. He'd been asked if he had any other connections to Uhl besides Rosenstein, and he'd said Benny Weiss. Then the voice had said Benny Weiss was dead, so he didn't have any other connection, and that was true. So here he was, and he was stuck.

Brock would come back someday, though. Maybe tomorrow, maybe next week. Even if he and the other guy were after the money, thirty-three grand wasn't enough to make him leave forever. He obviously had too many good things going already right around here.

So is that what Parker should do — stay here and wait for Brock to come back, the other guy to come back? If they brought the money with them, he'd take it away. If they didn't, he'd bend them until they told him where to find Uhl.

But that was so long and so chancy. If they had Uhl spooked, they could come back and not know anymore themselves where to find him. Or they could go up against Uhl and lose. Too many things could happen, with him sitting passive in this bombed-out apartment.

But what else was there to do? His only other link to Uhl was Benny Weiss, and Benny Weiss was dead.

Benny Weiss.

Parker stopped in his tracks. Benny Weiss. Maybe, after all....

The things he wanted from here he packed into a paper bag from the kitchen, and then he made his way through the mess to the front door and out. He was moving fast again.

Seven

The porch was full of children. Parker went up the stoop and through them to the front door, and they stopped swinging on the glider, climbing on the railing, playing soldiers on the floor, and stared at him. He stood at the screen door, looking through it into the mohair dimness of the living room, and pushed the bell button. An Avon-calling chime rang far away in the kitchen. The children were silent and wide-eyed behind him, staring at his back because he was something new.

The woman who appeared at the far end of the living room, drying her hands on her apron, was short and round and dowdy, with fluffy gray hair and a faded dress and down-at-the-heel slippers. "Coming," she called. "Coming." She scuffed across the living room carpet peering through her glasses at him. Framed in the doorway he had to be a silhouette to her, unidentifiable until she got close, and he saw the instant she recognized him. Her step faltered; her hands stopped moving in the apron; her mouth got a sudden slack look to it. Then she became more brisk again, saying, "Parker. I never thought to see you here." She pushed open the screen door. "Come on in. You kids keep it down, now."

A half a dozen of them shouted, "Yes, Mrs. Weiss!" and the racket that Parker had interrupted suddenly started up again.

Parker stepped into the house, and she let the screen door shut behind them. She said, "We'll be able to hear ourselves think in the kitchen. Besides, I've got some baking to watch."

"All right."

He followed her through the small, neat, overstuffed rooms

to the kitchen, which was large and square and expensively equipped and full of bakery aromas. Three glass cookie jars along the back of one counter were all full, each with a different kind of cookie.

"Sit down," she said. "Do you want coffee?"

She wouldn't know about her husband yet, and it would help her if she was doing something when he told her, so he said, "Thanks."

"Just a jiffy," she said. Turning her back to him to start the coffee, she said, "You being here is bad news, I suppose. You being here, Benny not being here."

"Yes."

"He's dead, I suppose."

"Yes."

She sagged forward for a second, her hands bracing her against the counter. He watched her, knowing she was trying to be as stoic and matter-of-fact as she could, knowing she would hate him to do anything to help her unless she was actually fainting or otherwise breaking down, and knowing that she had to have rehearsed this moment for years, ever since the first time Benny had gone away for a month on a job. Like Claire, Parker's own woman. Rehearsing the way she would handle it when she got the news. If she got the news. When she got the news.

There was a long, taut second when it could go either way—she could fall to the floor or go on making the coffee—and then she sighed, a long, shuddering sound, and shifted her weight and reached for the coffeepot. Still with her back to him, hands busy making the coffee, she said, "That wouldn't be why you're here. Not just to tell me about it. You aren't the type, Parker. You never were, you never will be."

"That's right," Parker said.

"You're strictly business," she said.

"I didn't kill him," Parker said. "Don't take it out on me."

She stopped what she was doing and just stood there for a minute. Then, in a muffled voice, she said, "Excuse me," and hurried from the room, keeping her face turned away from him.

He made the coffee himself, a full pot, and then sat down at the table again to wait. When the coffee was done perking he poured himself a cup and was sitting at the table drinking it when she came back into the room. She was red-eyed, and her face looked puffier than before. There was a pinched look around her eyes and a strained, artificial smile on her mouth. "You were right," she said. "I shouldn't take it out on you."

She got herself a cup from the cupboard, poured coffee, and sat down across the table from him. "So what is it you want?"

"Do you know a guy named George Uhl?"

"George? Young?"

"About thirty."

"Thin hair on top. Black hair. And kind of tall and skinny."

"That's the one," Parker said.

"Benny brought him around a couple of times," she said. "I never got his last name, just the George part."

"Do you know where he came from? How I get in touch with him?"

She shook her head thoughtfully. "No, I don't think so. Benny just brought him around once or twice. Wasn't he with you people this time?"

"Yeah, he was."

She looked closely at him. "Did he do something? Is that it?"

Parker nodded.

"Something that caused what happened to Benny?"

"Yes."

She frowned, trying to understand things, and took the time to sip some coffee. Then she said, "You aren't the revenge type, Parker, not if there's nothing in it for you. What do you want with this boy?"

Parker said, "He crossed us. He shot your husband in the head. He killed the other guy in the job, and he tried to kill me. And he took off with the money."

"Oh," she said. "The money."

"That's what I want," Parker said.

"But you don't have any way to find this George, is that it?"

"Not if you can't help me."

"I can see that," she said. She drank some more coffee and then said, "But if you could have found him without me, I never would have seen you at all. Seen you or heard a word from you."

"That's right," Parker said.

"Some of the money belongs to me now," she said.

Parker shook his head. "Come off it," he said. "Some things you don't inherit."

"Not unless I can help you," she said.

"That's right. You want a cut, is that it?"

"Half," she said.

"No."

"If there's just you left," she said, "then half that money belongs to me."

"Wrong. Phil Andrews left people, too. He's got a cut coming."

"Are you going to give it to them?"

"No. But I'm not going to give his share to you either. Benny would have had a quarter of the pie if things had worked out. That would be somewhere between seven and eight thousand."

"What do you mean, seven or eight thousand? Benny told me he'd be coming back with fifteen."

"That was a top estimate. We ran into bad luck and got about as little as we could. Benny ever overestimate in front before?"

She nodded grudgingly. "All right, all the time. But when he told me fifteen I thought sure he'd come back with ten or twelve."

"So did we, but it didn't work out that way."

She frowned, thinking it over, then suddenly started and cried, "My baking!" She jumped to her feet, grabbed a potholder, and opened the oven. Out came the two halves of layer cake, smelling hot and fresh. She put them on the counter to cool and turned off the oven. Then she put the potholder down, turned back to Parker, and said, "I couldn't trust you worth a damn. Don't you think I don't know that? You'd never come back here with the money."

"I have two thousand cash in my pocket I can give you," he said. "Or I can give you my word I'll come back with a quarter of whatever I get. Which do you want?"

She glanced up at the kitchen clock, biting her lip. "I wish my brother was around," she said. "He'd know what I should do."

"Call him."

"He's out on his rounds." She came back to the table and sat down. "Give me the two thousand as an advance."

He shook his head. "One or the other," he said. "Not both. What did Benny say about me? He ever say anything to you about me?"

"I know, I know," she said. "I know what Benny thought of you. *He* could trust you. That doesn't mean I can trust you."

"Why not?"

"Benny was a fellow professional."

'You're his widow."

She made a crooked smile. When she talked with him her expressions were at variance with her appearance, the gray hair and the apron and the slippers and the cake in the oven. A very sharp and worldly woman existed down inside the Apple Mary exterior. She said, "Sentiment, Parker?"

He shrugged. "Make up your mind, Grace," he said. "If you don't know anything I'll have to root around somewhere else."

"Do you have somewhere else?"

"I can just keep asking people in the business till I find somebody who knows George Uhl."

"That could take a while."

"That's why I'm here."

She studied him, then said, "Let me see the two thousand."

He took a roll of bills held with a rubber band from his side jacket pocket. He slid the rubber band onto his wrist and counted out two thousand dollars onto the kitchen table. There were a few bills left, and these he put in his wallet, then rolled the two thousand and put the rubber band around it. "It's right here," he said and put it back in his pocket.

"All right," she said. "Let me make a phone call or two. I'll be right back." She got to her feet.

Parker said, "Why not just give me the names and let me make my own calls?"

"These are people who'll talk to me, not you."

"All right. Go ahead."

She left the room, and Parker got up to pour himself another cup of coffee. He sat at the table again, listening to the children yelling and running around out front, smelling the smells of cake and cookies, looking through doorways at small, snug neat rooms. Grace Weiss, childless herself, with a heavy heistman for a husband, had turned herself into a kind of nursery-rhyme mother image, the cake and the cookie lady at whose house all the children of the neighbourhood congregated.

Parker had been here a couple of times before, and he remembered how Benny too had built himself a completely different at-home image. He was the semi-retired putterer, the Little League umpire, the maker of model planes and pup tents with the neighbourhood boys, the constructor of birdhouses and clipper of hedges, a vague and amiable little man in baggy pants, with his glasses slipping down his nose. The difference was so complete that the first time Parker had come here he hadn't recognized Weiss and had then thought Weiss had changed so much, grown too old, and couldn't be used anymore. But Weiss had let him know he was still his old self on the job, and he was.

Parker knew that he himself was different when he wasn't working. More relaxed, a little slower in moving, a little more vocal. But the differences were minor compared with those Benny and Grace Weiss had managed.

It was fifteen minutes before Grace came back, and when she did she had a folded slip of paper in her hand. She sat down across the table from Parker again, took a sip of her cold coffee, and said, "Nobody knows Benny's dead, so I just let them all think I was calling on his account. I didn't say anything about you or anything else."

"Good."

She looked at the slip of paper in her hand, then at Parker. "I decided I want the two thousand," she said. "Not because I don't trust you, Parker, but because I don't know what can happen. It's too much of a chance. Benny left me insurance, but how do I collect before I get official word he's dead?"

"You won't," Parker told her.

"That's wonderful," she said. "So now I have to wait seven years for an Enoch Arden. What do I live on in the meantime?"

"Benny salted some cash away."

"Sure he did. And this house is paid for, and everything in it is paid for. But he didn't salt that much away, and there's still living expenses. I don't have enough to last me seven years. And maybe you'd come back, maybe you really would, and give me seven thousand dollars. But maybe you wouldn't, or maybe you won't get the money, or maybe something will happen that neither one of us can forsee. So I'll take the two thousand. It's sure."

Parker took the roll out of his pocket again and put it in the middle of the table. She didn't touch it, but she reached out and put the slip of paper on the table beside it.

Parker picked up the paper and opened it, and written inside were two names and addresses, the first female, the second male. He looked at her.

She said, "The top one is the girl George was living with last year. That's her address; he used to live with her there. They split up a while ago, but she might still know where he is."

"All right. And the other one?"

"He and Benny and George were going to do something together once. It was his caper — he found it and planned it."

Parker tapped the paper. "This guy? Lewis Pearson?"

"Yes. It was Pearson's idea, and he brought Benny and George together. That's how Benny got to know George — when they were planning this other thing. But it never came off."

"Why not?"

"I don't know. Benny told me once he thought Pearson had

71

never been serious about it. I don't know what went wrong. But Pearson knows George."

"You try calling Pearson just now?"

"Yes. I told him Benny wanted to get in touch with George Uhl, and he said I should tell Benny to stay away from Uhl, he was no good. I couldn't push the question after that. Maybe you can."

"Maybe I can." Parker got to his feet. "Thanks, Grace."

"I did it for the money," she said.

Eight

After he rang the bell three times without getting an answer, Parker walked around on the smooth green lawn to the back of the house. It was a white ranch style, very new, on a plot big enough to make the neighbouring houses barely felt presences beyond the high hedges bordering the property. A white Mustang in the driveway meant somebody was home. It was a hot and sunny day here outside Alexandria, Virginia, so maybe they hadn't answered the bell because they were out back.

They were. The rear of the house was dominated by a turquoise swimming pool. A greased, bronze woman in a two-piece white bathing suit lay on a chaise longue in the sunlight, eyes closed behind sunglasses, and a bronzed, stocky man in black bathing trunks, with hairy shoulders, was swimming doggedly back and forth in the pool like a man being paid a small salary to do so many laps every day.

Parker stood beside the pool and neither of them noticed him. He watched the man swimming back and forth, and finally the man glanced up and saw him standing there and was so startled he sank for a second. He came spewing back to the surface and swam over to the edge of the pool, grabbing the tiles near Parker's feet. Looking up, squinting in the sunlight, he said, "Where the hell did you come from?"

"I rang the bell and didn't get any answer, so I came around."

"That damn thing. We never hear it out here."

The woman across the way had sat up and was looking at them.

Parker said, "Are you Lewis Pearson?"

"Yeah, that's me. You an insurance man? You don't look like one."

The woman called, "Who is it, Lew?"

He turned in the water, keeping one forearm on the tiles to support himself, and yelled, "How the hell do I know? Give me a minute, will ya?"

"You don't have to snap my head off!"

"Just butt outski for a minute."

Parker said to the top of his head, "I'm a friend of Benny Weiss."

Pearson turned around again, forgetting the woman, and squinted up at Parker once more. Thoughtfully he said, "You are, huh?"

"Yes."

"That's a funny coincidence. Hold on a minute, lemme get outa here."

Pearson turned away, pushing wearily off from the edge of the pool, and slogged across to the ladder on the other side. He pulled himself up out of the water, padded over to the empty chaise longue beside his woman, picked up a towel there, and began to pat himself dry. The woman said something to him; he said something back. She glanced over at Parker, said something else to Pearson, and he turned and called, "You want something to drink? Gin and tonic?"

Parker didn't want anything but information, but he'd learned a long time ago that people liked you more if you let them play host, and people would only tell you things if they liked you, so he said, "That'd be fine, Thank you."

The woman got up, ran a finger under the bottom of her bathing suit in back the way women do, stepped into sandals, and went off to the house. Parker walked around the pool towards Pearson, who was still drying himself, scrubbing vigorously with the white towel. He was of medium height, stocky build, about forty, and hairy all over, legs and arms and back and chest and shoulders. He finally tossed the towel back onto the chaise and said, "You want to stay out here or go inside in the air-conditioning?"

"It's up to you."

"Let's stay out here," Pearson said. "I'm working on my

tan."

He led the way to a table with a beach umbrella over it. Parker sat in the shaded chair and Pearson sat in sunlight. Pearson said, "I don't know all of Benny's friends. Which one are you?" He was being friendly and easygoing and relaxed, but Parker could see the eyes studying him, not yet having made up their mind about him.

"My name's Parker. I don't know if Benny ever mentioned me."

"Parker?" Pearson started a smile. "Yeah, Benny mentioned a guy named Parker. Once or twice. He thinks Parker's the best there is. In his kind of business, I mean."

"You're in the business, too," Parker said. "Anyway, you thought about it."

Wariness came back into Pearson's face. "I did? When was that?"

"The time you and Benny and George Uhl were going to do something together. Only it didn't work out."

Pearson didn't say anything. He studied Parker's face.

The woman came out with a tray containing iced drinks in tall blue glasses. She put it down and said to Pearson, "Business, Lew?"

"Yeah, I think so," he said. He sounded cautious, wary.

"I'll swim," she said.

"You do that," he said. He was keeping his eyes on Parker.

She went over and dove into the pool, and Parker said, "Benny's wife called you about nine-thirty this morning."

"She did?"

"I was in the house when she called you," Parker said. "She called you because I asked her to."

"She said it was for Benny."

"I know. It was simpler that way, to say Benny wanted to get in touch with Uhl. But all you'd say was Benny should stay away from Uhl."

Pearson frowned and picked up one of the drinks. "Yeah, I know I did," he said. "I thought about that later and I was sorry

I did that. It isn't up to me who Benny works with. He knows what I think of Uhl. Just because I've got my own personal hack about George Uhl doesn't mean I should keep somebody else from getting in touch with him."

"What's your bitch about Uhl?"

Pearson glanced at Parker, at his drink, He turned his head and looked at his wife floating lazily in the pool. He shook his head and said, "It's a personal thing; it doesn't have anything to do with business at all. You aren't drinking your drink."

Parker took the other drink and sipped it, remembering Brock and the drugged coffee. But there wasn't going to be anything like that here; it didn't have the feeling about it.

He said, "Benny doesn't want to talk to Uhl. I do."

Pearson frowned. "You've got work for him?"

"I have a personal thing I've got to get settled with him."

Pearson gave a sour grin. "You too? Georgy does get around." He was facing the house, with Parker facing the opposite way, and now Pearson looked at the house and said, "I don't know."

"You don't know what?"

"That's why Grace called, huh? To get Uhl's address for you."

"Yes."

"So now you're coming to me direct," Pearson said, and then he said, "Uh," and a small black thing appeared in the middle of his forehead, making him look cross-eyed. His head started to go back, the black thing went deep, burrowing, turning red at the edges, and the sound of the shot finally caught up with it, a flat, echoless clap in the middle of the sunshine.

Parker dove off the chair. Things speeded up all at once, shots were sounding one on top of the other, Parker was rolling across flagstone and green lawn, the world was full of spinning confusion. Then he was in the shadow of the hedge and he could lie flat on his stomach, peering out, the smell of grass and dirt in his nostrils, the air surprisingly cool down here in the shadow of the hedge. Far away, Pearson's body was still falling out of the chair, as though that little space existed in slow motion with the rest of the world boiling around it at top speed.

Parker had one of his guns in his hip pocket. He dragged it out and watched the house. There weren't any more shots coming from there.

Pearson's body landed. It made a soft mound on the flagstones.

Parker got to his hands and knees and began crawling along the line of hedge, coming indirectly closer to the house.

The woman's head appeared up over the edge off the pool, staring at the body lying there. She began to scream.

Parker got to his feet and ran for a corner of the house. There were no more shots. He moved quickly down the side of the house, but then he heard a car door slam somewhere out front. He ran and got to the front of the house in time to see a pale blue Chevy disappearing away to the right. Uhl's car.

He could hear the woman still screaming. Go back there? No, she wasn't going to know anything, and a hysterical woman could be several kinds of unexpected trouble.

Parker knew what had happened; he could see the whole thing clear and entire. Pearson had told him about having second thoughts after refusing to tell Grace Weiss how to get in touch with Uhl. So he'd done something about the second thoughts, but instead of calling Grace back he'd gone directly to Uhl.

Uhl must have had a bad minute there when Pearson called him and told him Benny Weiss wanted to see him. But then Uhl had to have worked it out and realized it meant Parker was after him. And he'd almost settled for Parker at the same time.

Where would Uhl go now? Pearson hadn't gotten around to telling Parker how to find Uhl, but Uhl couldn't know that or take a chance on it. So now he'd dig a hole someplace and climb in and pull the dirt in after him. Now he was going to be twice as tough to find.

And Parker had only one name and address left. Joyce Langer, 154 West 87th Street, New York City.

Pearson's wife was still screaming. Parker got into his car and drove away from there.

Nine

The girl who opened the door to Parker's knock had the aggrieved look of the born loser. Without it, she would have been good-looking. A willowy girl with long chestnut hair streaming down her back in the manner of urban folk singers, she had good brown eyes and a delicately boned face, but the hangdog expression destroyed her shot at beauty. You looked at her and you knew right away her voice would be a whine.

It was. She said, "What is it? I'm having dinner."

It was eight o'clock, a little late for dinner if she was by herself, and from her clothing Parker guessed she was by herself. She was in wrinkled dark blue bell-bottom slacks, rope-sole sandals, and a gray sweatshirt with a cartoon character's face on it.

Parker said, "I want to talk to you about George Uhl."

Her face hardened, the complainer lines deepening in her forehead and around her mouth. "I haven't seen George for over a year," she said. "Try somewhere else."

"Where?"

"I wouldn't know," she said, and started to close the door.

Parker stuck his foot in the entrance. "Just a minute," he said.

She looked at the foot as though she couldn't believe it, and when she looked back up at Parker her complainer's face was on her so strong she looked as though she had a toothache. She said, "What do you think you're doing?" And the whine had gone up an octave.

"You don't like George Uhl," he said.

"What does it matter to you who I like? Do you want me to call for help?"

"I don't like George either," Parker said. "If I find him, I'll cause him some trouble."

She looked at him appraisingly. "You will?"

"Yes."

"What is this? You a jealous husband or something?"

"Something."

She looked past Parker at the hall, frowning, and then half turned to look at the apartment behind her. "I was just having dinner . . . ."

"I'll wait."

"The apartment's a sight."

"I couldn't care less," he said.

She looked at him again. "You're really mad at George?"

"Yes."

She hesitated a second longer, then shrugged and pulled the door all the way open, saying, "Okay, come on in." Even that was said as though a heavy weight had just been put on her.

Parker walked into a sloppy living room, with a TV dinner on the coffee table and the television on with the sound turned low. He stood there and she shut the door after him, saying, "I don't like fuss when it's just me. You know how it is." She was embarrassed about herself, though Parker didn't care, and her embarrassment wouldn't make her change anything.

"I know how it is," Parker agreed.

She came around him, looking forlornly at her dinner. "It's probably cold anyway. Listen — uh. What did you say your name was?"

"Tom Lynch."

"Hi, Tom. I'm Joyce Langer." It looked for a second as though she would even offer to shake hands with him.

"I know," he said.

"Listen," she said, trying to be animated. "Have you had dinner?"

Parker had driven straight up from Alexandria with stops only for gas. Four hours ago he'd had some of Lew Pearson's gin and tonic, but nothing since. He said, "No, I haven't."

"Then why don't you take me? I know a pretty nice little

Mexican place down on Seventy-ninth Street. Okay?"

Parker was feeling the sense of urgency more than ever now. The people he was talking to were spread out up and down the eastern seaboard; he was wasting most of his time driving from one city to another. In the meantime Uhl could be anywhere. And Rosenstein could still be ahead of him.

But Joyce Langer could close up on him at any second, and he knew it. She was an injustice collector, a whiner, a stubborn, ineffectual hater. She might not be able to tell him a damn thing, but he would have to keep her happy until he found out one way or the other, so he said, "Okay. Let's go."

"Just let me change," she said, and in her animation she almost did look pretty, the complainer lines fading though not entirely disappearing. "I won't be a sec," she said.

Parker knew that meant ten minutes, maybe fifteen. "All right," he said.

"You could watch television — that's a pretty good show on there right now. A special about the Verrazano Narrows Bridge. You want me to turn it up?"

"I'll take care of it."

"Let me just get rid of . . . ." Her words trailed off as she picked up the TV dinner and hurried with it from the room.

Parker sat where his eyes would be attracted to the television set, but he didn't turn the sound up. The movement on the screen — Girders lifting, men in work helmets looking up and moving their arms — distracted him slightly, and for the rest he just made himself be patient.

He knew too little about Uhl, that was the problem. Too little about Uhl and too little about the people around him. He had to poke around blind in Uhl's life, never knowing what the reaction would be. With Rosenstein he'd succeeded only in setting another wolf on the scent. Pearson would have been good, because he had a sexual complaint against Uhl, but all that time spent driving down to Alexandria had played to Uhl's advantage, and now Parker was back almost to the beginning again. The last link to Uhl's life, a discarded girl friend. With

Uhl spooked and Rosenstein prowling around somewhere.

The point was, thirty-three thousand dollars wasn't enough to drive Uhl out of his life. He hadn't planned, obviously, on taking the thirty-three grand and going to Europe or Canada or South America with it. It wasn't enough. He'd counted on getting rid of all his partners in the robbery, and then he could go back into his normal life with four times his share and nobody to notice anything or ask him anything. Parker's being alive had spoiled things for him, but he still couldn't just abandon his life. He didn't have enough money for it. If Parker — or Rosenstein — spooked him enough he might finally take off just out of desperation, hoping to start up somewhere else again with the thirty-three thousand as a stake. But what Uhl was going to want to do was hang around the general area, out of sight, until it had all blown over, until Parker and Rosenstein had given up and gone on to other things. And in the meantime Uhl would want to maintain some sort of contact with his regular life to know what was happening, if for no other reason.

Pearson was proof of that. There'd been someone, some individual person, that Pearson could call and get to deliver a message to Uhl. That someone, or maybe a different someone now, could lead Parker to Uhl. All he needed was to be led to the someone.

Which meant he had to get into Uhl's life, had to make contact with the people Uhl knew. And all he had left to help him was one old girl friend with a hate against Uhl and a complaint against the world.

She was back in ten minutes, and she'd tried her best. She was in a yellow sleeveless miniskirted dress with orange Mondrian lines, her shoes were casual flats in a matching orange, and she carried a small orange handbag. She'd brushed her hair and made up her face and even put on eyelashes. The whiner was well disguised now; if you didn't look close, you might miss her.

Except for the voice. "There!" she said. "That didn't take long, did it?" Even through the animation the petulant overtones remained.

"Not long," Parker said.

She switched off the television set, and they left the apartment. They were on 87th Street between Amsterdam and Columbus, and she led the way over to Amsterdam and then south.

Parker tried once or twice to get her to talk about Uhl as they walked along, but she wouldn't do it. "Not on an empty stomach," she said, and made stupid conversation about the weather instead. "Isn't this weather something? Boy! Different every day. What about that rainstorm yesterday? Wasn't that something?"

"Yes," Parker said. He was thinking that a lot of time had gone by and he hadn't gotten anywhere. They'd knocked over the bank on Monday, and it was Thursday before he'd gotten to Brock, the day it rained. Now it was Friday. Four days of running back and forth, and Uhl was still out there someplace, sitting on the money.

The restaurant had an aquarium decorating scheme — fish and fishnets, candles flickering on the tables. They ate Mexican food, cooling their mouths with beer, and afterwards over coffee Parker said, "Now we talk about George Uhl."

"Do you have a match?"

He held a light for her, and she cupped her hand around his while she lit her cigarette. "Mm, thank you." She smiled at him through smoke and candlelight. "You have strong hands. And a one-track mind. George is all you're interested in, isn't he?"

"For now," Parker said because he thought he ought to play her game with her just a little. He didn't want her to freeze.

"I don't know what you have against George," she said, looking down at the ashtray as she flicked no ashes from her cigarette, "But I have plenty."

"I won't pry into your personal life," Parker told her, short-circuiting a long, sad story. "All I want is to find out where he is."

She looked at him and frowned a little. She was being

coquettish now, even frowning coquettishly, and with that and the dimness of the candlelight and the cigarette smoke the whiner was almost completely out of sight. Except for the voice. "I haven't seen him for a year," she said. "I honestly haven't. More than a year."

"You used to know him," Parker said.

"Didn't I, though," she said, twisting her mouth scornfully.

"So you knew the people he knew. You knew his friends."

"A man like George," she said, "doesn't have friends. Just people he uses."

"That could be. But some people think they're his friends. Everybody has somebody who thinks he's his friend."

She shrugged, flicking ashes again. "I suppose so."

"They're the ones who'll know where he is. But I don't know yet who *they* are."

She looked at him abruptly with something very pained behind her eyes. "How did you hear about me?"

"From a woman named Grace Weiss."

The name obviously meant nothing to her. She said, "Who on earth is she?"

"The wife of a guy George knew."

"How did she know anything about me?"

"I don't know."

The complainer crept a little more into the open. "I don't like the idea of people talking about me. People I don't even know."

"She told me you used to know George. That's all she said. And if you used to know him, you know some of his friends."

"I suppose."

"Who would they be?" Parker asked her.

She would have liked to dwell on the injustice of strangers talking about her, but she came around reluctantly to consider Parker's question. She said, "It's been a while. George and I never really were that close anyway. He just used me, the way he uses everybody. He doesn't let anybody get close to him, not really close."

She wouldn't stay on the track. Parker nudged her back on,

84

saying, "But you had to know some of the other people he knew."

"Well, there was Howie; that's one."

"Howie. You know his last name?"

"Something Italian. Let me think. It was like coffee, you know, the instant coffee? What is it, espresso. Progressi, that was his name! Howie Progressi."

"Where's he live?"

"Oh, somewhere in Brooklyn. He has a garage down there. He and George are both car nuts. Howie enters those demolition derby things out on the Island. You know the kind of thing?"

"No. Demolition derby?"

"A lot of crazy guys get into beat-up cars," she said, "and they all go out in the middle and bump into each other. It's supposed to be a gas, but frankly I never saw that much in it. I went with George a couple of times, and it was just creepy. Everybody in the stands screaming and yelling and cheering, and these crazy guys out there in the middle of the track bumping into each other. And the last car still moving is the winner. Is that creepy? And they talk about they wonder if this country's violent. Wow."

"And Howie Progressi drives in these things?"

"All the time. He never wins or anything, but he doesn't even want to win, if you ask me. He's just there to bump into other cars. He and George were buddies for a while. I don't know if they are still."

"And you don't know his address?"

"Just somewhere in Brooklyn." She shrugged. "I suppose he's in the phone book."

"All right. Who else?"

"There was somebody named Barry he used to see sometimes. I never met him, and then he moved to Washington or someplace."

Washington? Near Alexandria. Uhl had been close enough to get to Pearson within a couple of hours, depending on what time

Pearson had his change of heart and contacted Uhl. Parker said, "Who is this Barry?"

"I don't know. That's all I ever heard was Barry. No last name or anything. I remember him and Howie talking about this Barry together one time and giggling like crazy. Because they had a secret, you know. They knew Barry and I didn't. That was supposed to be funny."

"Howie knows Barry, though, is that right?"

"Sure. They had a lot of fun over that one."

"Anybody else?"

"There was a cop," she said. "I never met him either, but Geroge saw him sometimes. They had something going on. I don't know what."

"What was his name?"

"Dumpke, or Drumpke. Dugald?" She frowned, rubbing the lines in her forehead with one finger. "Dumek!" she cried. "That's it, Dumek!" She spelled it.

"What's his first name?"

"I don't know. George always just called him Officer Dumek. He'd say, 'I've got to go see Officer Dumek.' Wait, I did see him one time. We went to the movies, up to the New Yorker, you know? On Broadway? And we were walking back and there was a police car stopped by a fire hydrant and there was nobody behind the wheel, but there was a policeman on the right side, sitting there with his arm out the window, and when we went by he waved and said, 'Hi, George.' And George said hi back, but I forget what name he said. But then he told me that was Officer Dumek. But I couldn't describe him or anything. He was just a policeman in a police car at night. You know?"

Parker nodded. "Okay. Anybody else?"

"Nope." She shook her head, being totally positive.

"Maybe somebody you haven't thought of?"

"I don't think so," she said. "I'm pretty sure not."

Parker gave it up. He said, "If he was in trouble, do you think he'd come to you?"

"Oh, I wish he would," she said savagely.

86

"Yeah, but would he?"

"I don't know. He's so damn arrogant, I suppose he might. If he didn't have anybody else to turn to, maybe he would. Think he could just walk back in and take over again." The whine was as sharp as vinegar now, the lines in her forehead looking like pencil strokes, crayon stokes, in the candlelight. Then she leaned forward and said, "You're really mad at him, aren't you?"

"Yes."

"You'd really beat him up, wouldn't you?"

It was what she wanted to hear, so he said, "Yes."

"I tell you what," she said, her voice dropping, becoming more confidential. "If I hear from George at all, I'll call you. Okay?"

Parker considered the offer. Was there anything else under it? No, he didn't thing so. He said, "All right. That'd be good."

"And if I think of anybody else, anything else that might help you, I'll call. Like Officer Dumek's first name, or anything like that."

"Good. You can reach me at the Rilington Hotel, in midtown. You know of it?"

"Rilington Hotel. I can look it up in the phone book."

"Right. I'm in and out of there, so if I'm not registered when you call, just tell them to hold the message for me."

She nodded. "You're from out of town, then, is that it?"

"I'm in New York a lot of the time," he told her to keep her interest alive.

It did. "Then maybe we can get to know each other a little," she said. "I could show you around the city some, if you don't know it very well."

"After I find George," he said.

"A one-track mind," she said, smiling. "I told you that's what you had."

"That's what I have."

She looked off toward the fishnets on the wall. "I wonder where George is," she said.

THREE

One

A second too late, George Uhl realized he'd shot the wrong man first. Weiss was falling, Andrews was lunging for a gun he was never going to be able to reach, but Parker was going out the window. It was Parker he should have taken out first, and then Andrews, with the old man last. Old men are slower.

Later on, thinking about it, he finally came to the conclusion that he'd shot Weiss first because he knew Weiss. Stupid subconscious thinking — deal with friends before you deal with strangers. But that was the only explanation, and it screwed things up all around.

If it hadn't been for Andrews, Uhl would have gotten Parker anyway, even though he'd gone for the wrong man first. But if he'd spent those extra few seconds getting Parker, Andrews would have had that gun in his hand and it might have gone the wrong way. So he had to take care of Andrews and let Parker go on out the window.

He was rattled for a while after that, and who wouldn't have been? The tension of the robbery, driving back, waiting for the right moment to throw down on the other three — he'd been wound up like a watch, and of course as soon as something went wrong in the plans he got hopelessly strung up for a couple of minutes.

Until he saw Parker's gun lying outside the window in the dust, and that was such a good break it almost made up for the stupidity. Anyway, it got him back on the track, and even though Parker got away into the woods Uhl was all right again, ready to go on with his plans. He was too smart to go crashing around in the woods after Parker. He'd have to let the bastard go.

But it wasn't all that bad. Parker and Uhl didn't know each

other, so how could Parker make trouble for him later on even if he wanted to? And besides, since Uhl was going to leave him unarmed and on foot out here, he was more than likely to be picked up by the cops. Let Parker do twenty years in a federal pen somewhere and *then* come looking for Uhl.

So he went on with his original plan, ignoring Parker's unscheduled existence. He went back and arranged for the fire, piling all the flammable stuff in the middle of the house, and then stacked the bodies on top so they'd burn thoroughly, first kicking their teeth loose. These bodies weren't going to be identified by fingerprints or dental records. These bodies weren't going to be identified.

In the barn he splashed gasoline around, led a trail of gasoline-soaked rags to Andrews' Mercury. Then he set the two fires and got out of there. Good-bye, Parker. Good-bye, Weiss and Andrews.

Number six. This was job number six, and from the first one he'd wanted to do this. Every time the job would be done, he'd drive the car to the hideout, the money would be split up, and he'd look at the piles of cash, he'd look at the fraction he was given, and he'd want it all. But every time there'd been something wrong. Too many men, or men he knew too well who had friends who knew him and would come after him. It took till job number six before the situation was right. Only three others in the heist, and he really didn't know any of them. Only Benny Weiss, and that not very much, just through organizing a job that didn't come off one time.

And was thirty-three thousand better than eight thousand? Was the extra twenty-five grand worth the risk? Uhl grinned to himself as he drove east.

But as he thought it over, he began to realize that the loose end of Parker could make a lot of trouble. If Parker wasn't picked up by the law, if he managed to get out from under, he would come looking for Uhl, and that was sure. Could he find him? Uhl didn't know. He wanted to think it couldn't be done, but he just wasn't sure.

All right. So the thing to do was lay low for a while. Wait and see if Parker popped up anywhere; wait and see if there were any other repercussions. If everything was quiet, in a week or two he could come out of hiding and everything would be the same. If there was trouble, he could stay hidden out and decide what to do about it.

The question was, Where to hide? He thought of Howie Progressi first because he knew Howie would get a kick out of the story of his taking the thirty-three grand from three sure old professionals, but almost as soon as he thought of Howie he rejected him again. For two reasons. First, everybody knew he and Howie were tight. If Parker came looking, one of the early people he'd see would be Howie. And second, if Howie learned about the thirty-three thousand, the bastard might try to take it away from him himself.

The next one he thought of was Joyce Langer. There was the advantage there that they'd split up over a year ago, so nobody was likely to look for him around her now. Also, he could pretty well control her, keep her under his thumb. But on the other hand she was such a goddam kvetch, and if somebody came around to make him trouble she might just blow the whistle on him to get back at him if she was feeling put-upon. And she was always feeling put-upon.

Barri? No, too many people knew he was shacked up with Barri Dane these days. If he tried staying at her place, and if Parker *did* come prowling around, Barri was one of the people he'd get to first.

He was into Pennsylvania when he remembered Ed Saugherty. He hadn't seen Ed since that time four or five years ago when the shmuck had called him: "Hi, George, it's Ed Saugherty. Remember me? I'm just in New York for a couple of days with a convention. I thought I'd look up my old high-school buddy."

Old high-school buddy. In those days George Uhl had been a big shot, a big wheel. High school had been great, the greatest part of his life so far, and in those days he'd had a half dozen little punks that hung around him, tagged after him, bought him beers, laughed at his jokes, listened to his stories about making out. And Ed Saugherty had been one of them, a round-faced stocky kid with red cheeks and thick glasses, an eager kid who liked to laugh and who loved to hear George's tough-sounding stories.

They'd met twice after that phone call, before Ed went back home to Philadelphia. He was working for a computer company now. He wore a white shirt and a tie even when he didn't have to, and the company had transferred him a few years before to Philadelphia. He'd made George very uncomfortable during both those meetings, and in fact after the first one — a couple hours' drinking together in a bar, with Ed picking up the tab, paying for it with a credit card — George had been sure Ed felt contempt for him now, thought of him as a loser. Ed had done a lot of talking about the company, his job, his future, his wife and children, his home in Philadelphia, his whole happy, successful life, and when he'd asked what George was doing now the only answer had been, "This and that. I get along."

But then Ed called him again the next day, and it turned out the old hero-worship was still very much alive. When George realized that Ed saw himself as a dull wage-slave and George as a guy with an exciting life, there was nothing for it but to agree with Ed completely and start playing the role to the hilt. That second meeting had been full of wild stories, a few of them true, a few of them invented, a lot of them adapted from paperback novels, and there was no question but that Ed would pick up the tab again. And though George had really been in tough money shape just then, the main reason he tapped Ed for a loan was because he understood that Ed's myth-comprehension of him demanded it. Ed pressed the forty bucks on him with a smile of absolute joy, saying, "No hurry about paying this back, George, no hurry about paying this back."

Was Ed Saugherty the man to go to now? Somebody he'd had no contact with at all in four or five years, and no real extended contact with for closer to twelve years. But somebody who'd do whatever George asked. Like giving him a perfect place to hide out.

So Philadelphia was where he went, and he found Ed living in a brick ranch-style house on a winding black-top street in a wellto do green suburb west of the city. It looked like a standard family in a standard setting, and George had no inclination to scratch the surface and see what was underneath. From the time he walked up the back to the driveway past the overturned tricycle to the open garage door where Ed was pouring gasoline into a power mower, George had no more interest in the people and the place than if they were the background for a television commercial.

"Ed, I'm in trouble. I need some help. I can't talk about it, but I need someplace to hide out for a few days."

Ed had fallen into his role in the melodrama as though he'd been rehearsing for it all his life. And why not? Didn't he see it two or three times a week on television? Didn't the situation keep cropping up, and wasn't his role always the same? The true friend, the ally, the last desperate hope of the hero. If he couldn't be the hero himself — and in going with the computer company, the wife, the brick house on the winding street, Ed had consciously turned his back on ever being the hero — this was the best possible supporting role.

Ed had a wife named Pam, a good-looking, slender woman in stretch pants, and she knew her role, too. She was against him, opposed to his staying there, opposed to Ed "getting involved," insistent on Ed finding out what George's true situation really was. George kept out of her way and left it up to Ed to handle her, never doubting for a minute that Ed would.

They had a guest room, and George kept to it most of the time. He made a halfhearted attempt to become pals with Ed's oldest son, a ten-year-old named Bob, but Bob wasn't interested, and George had been strictly making the gesture because he felt the situation expected it of him. After that he stayed close to the guest room except for the strained, silent mealtimes with Ed giving him sheepish smiles and Pam pointedly ignoring him and the two younger kids staring at him with their faces smeared with mashed potato.

The important thing was to find out if there was going to be any trouble from Parker or from anybody else, so what he needed was a link to his normal life, somebody he could trust, and that was Barri. He called her Tuesday afternoon, gave her an abridged version of the situation, told her the phone number here but nothing else about the place, and she agreed to relay any messages that might come in but not to give anybody any information about him. Then he sat back to wait.

He didn't hear from Barri till Thursday, and then it was to say Matt Rosenstein wanted to get in touch with him and had left a D.C. number. George had worked with Rosenstein on two jobs, and they'd both been involved in the abort where he'd met Benny Weiss. Would his calling now be a coincidence? It had to be, but George was wary. Rosenstein was based in New York, so why a number in Washington? Why was he so close to George's stamping grounds and to Barri?

He called Rosenstein, and Rosenstein gave him a long story about a caper he was organizing, something absolutely safe and with a fat return. Rosenstein wanted to meet with him and talk it over.

George didn't specifically doubt Rosenstein, but he didn't trust him either. His wariness, and the thirty-three thousand dollars tucked away in a suitcase in the guest room closet, kept him uninterested in Rosenstein's offer. He said so, but Rosenstein kept pressing, kept wanting to have a meeting with him, until George began to get actively suspicious, at which point Rosenstein abruptly gave up, told him he was missing a sure winner, and hung up.

That was yesterday, and ever since that call George had been uneasy. He sensed people moving around out there, somewhere beyond the range of his sight and hearing, prowling around, up to something. He was getting nervous.

And then late this morning Barri had called again, and the message this time almost made him drop the receiver. "Benny

Weiss wants to get in touch with you."

"Wait! Wait, wait, wait!"

"What's the matter, George?"

All he could do was keep saying *wait*. He was standing in Ed's living room; he was alone in the house; there was silence and springtime outside, sunlight and grass. He had to get his mind back inside his head, and until then all he could do was say *wait*.

Finally he found a question he could ask: "Who called you? He called you himself?"

"No. A guy named Lew Pearson called. He said he was passing the message on."

Lew Pearson. That bastard. Wouldn't he like to do George a favour, though. "I'll call you back," he said and hung up and prowled the house a while, trying to make up his mind.

What did it mean? Benny Weiss was dead. Parker? How would Parker get to Lew Pearson? Through Benny's wife maybe. So were Pearson and Parker combining against him? Was Pearson spilling his guts to Parker about everything he knew? Or was Pearson taking over from Parker, or running something on his own?

Maybe they were all in it together, Pearson and Rosenstein and Parker. Closing in on him.

He couldn't just stand around here. He'd been jittery since the call yesterday; he'd wanted to move, act, do something, but there hadn't been anything to do.

Now there was something to do. Nip Pearson in the bud.

He left a note for Ed on the kitchen table. He considered taking the money, but it would be safer here and finally he left it. And then he headed south.

A little over three hours later he was at Pearson's house. He rang the bell, got no answer, found the door unlocked, and worked his way silently through the house, pistol in his hand. Then he looked out a back window and saw Lew sitting out there with a bathing suit on, Madge drifting around in the pool.

Ask questions? Did he want to know what was going on? No, he knew what was going on. There was only one meaning for

Pearson's message: He'd been trying to rattle George, make George expose himself by doing something stupid. And there was a quick way to defend himself.

He opened the window a couple of inches and knelt on the floor. He braced his gun hand on the sill, and he never saw the guy in the other chaise longue until after he'd shot Pearson. That chaise was facing the other way. There was nothing showing but the top of a head, and that was easy not to see at this distance. And Pearson had acted like a man alone, sitting there sipping his drink.

But then George fired his first shot, and the other man erupted out of the other chaise, and damned if it wasn't Parker again. George emptied his pistol at the son of a bitch, but Parker rolled like a cat across the lawn and got clean away.

Would nothing stop him? This was George's second try at him, and he'd failed again.

"The next time," George muttered, "I take my first shot at *you.*" Then he got to his feet and hustled out of there.

Two

Barri Dane stood by the door, smiling at her students as they trickled out bravely to face the day. She shut the door behind the last of them and the smile fell from her face like a picture off a wall. When she walked across the bare floor of the rehearsal room her reflection kept pace with her in the wall-length mirror on her right, but she didn't bother to look at it. She knew what she looked like in black leotards, she knew the twenty-eight-year-old body was as firm and slender and well-curved as the eighteen-year-old body had been, she knew that the twenty-eight-year-old face looked tougher and more knowing and more provocative than the eighteen-year-old face had looked, and she knew the fatigue she was feeling would show only in a slight slump of the shoulders, a slight flat-footedness in the walk. So she walked the length of a twenty-two-foot mirror without glancing in it once, went through a curtained doorway into the living quarters of the building, turned on the shower water in the bathroom, and then stripped out of the leotard in the bedroom while waiting for the water to run hot.

Washington, D.C., is a tough town for the young single woman, and that's because there are so many of them there. Government never has enough bureaucracy, and bureaucracy never has enough secretaries, stenographers, typists, and file clerks. So Washington is full of young women, and because there are so many of them a lot of them are lonely.

Barri Dane's current livelihood was a direct result of this loneliness. Although in the past she'd been a stripper, a con artist's shill, and a few other things, today she was an educator, a teacher with her own studio and with two well-attended classes every day.

It was part of her self-promotion when she said that the main thing she taught was confidence. "If you finish this course with new self-confidence," she always told new classes, "we will both have succeeded."

In more mundane terms, Barri Dane's course was a general study in physical education. There were classes in calisthenics and in hygiene, as well as classes in belly dancing, in modeling, and in judo. A student could sign up for a complete four-month course, two one-hour sessions a week, for one hundred fifty dollars, or she could select a shorter program devoting itself to any one of the subjects Barri taught, for smaller amounts of money. There was a good living in it and it was by far the cleanest and most legitimate means of earning a dollar she'd ever found for herself, but after nearly two years she was bored to death with the damn thing. Still, there was nothing much else to do, so she kept on with it.

The water was hot. She stepped in and started to soap and got to thinking about George Uhl. She knew he wasn't much; she'd always known that, just as she'd always known that she was invariably attracted to the George Uhl type, to the tough guys with a weakness, the big talkers who somehow would never come through. But George had just a little bit more going for him than those other bums; he had just enough strength so that he really did act every once in a while. And he'd acted now, all right. He'd done something and he was in it up to his neck. He wouldn't tell her about it when they talked on the phone, but she knew once she saw him again in the flesh she'd get the story out of him. She always did. And all she hoped was he hadn't dug himself into too deep a hole this time. Better a live bum than a dead hero.

She came out of the shower at last and toweled herself vigorously till her skin flushed red. Then she hung the towel over its bar to dry and went naked into the bedroom, where a man with a gun in his hand was sitting very casually on the edge of the bed.

He smiled at her. "That's a nice way to say hello, honey," he said.

100

She recognized him. He was the guy who'd come around yesterday wanting to get in touch with George. He'd given her a phone number to pass on to George, he'd said his name was Matt Rosenstein, and he'd left. When she'd told George about it he hadn't seemed upset. In fact he said something about calling Matt to see what he wanted.

Barri thought, *George, did you get me into something bad?* She said, "What do you want, Mac?"

"I want George," he said. He was medium height but very broad, massive in the shoulders and chest and neck like a weight lifter. He had a square head with a mean-looking face and a way of smiling that was somehow very nasty.

She said, "I told George you called. I gave him the number."

"I know you did, and that was real nice. But now I want George in person. I want to go talk to him."

The sight of the gun in his hand was making her feel very cold, but she was afraid if she went to put a robe on or anything he'd take it as a sign of weakness. She was terrified to show him weakness, as though he were a vicious dog that had to be faced down. She said, "I don't know where he is."

He got to his feet, taking his time, that nasty smile drooping on his face. "For your sake, honey," he said, "I hope that isn't the truth. Because I'm going to start on you now, and the only thing on God's earth that's going to make me stop is when you tell me where George is."

Three

Paul Brock sat on the floor in the middle of the living room, and tears streamed down his cheeks. He felt he couldn't go on; he felt it was all too much for him; he felt everything was lost and doomed and beyond recall. *I just don't have the energy,* he kept thinking.

Matt had told him to come back to the apartment at five o'clock on Friday afternoon, and Matt would phone him there. "Parker won't be hanging around there anymore by then," he said. "But keep an eye out for him anyway."

So that's what he'd done, coming downtown from the hotel half an hour early, both to be ahead of the worst of the rush hour and to have a little time in the apartment, and what had he walked into?

It was criminal. It was like murdering a person, what had been done here, just like beating the life out of a human being. The apartment had been raped, viciously, violently raped, and then kicked to death.

All the time he'd put into this place, all the time and thought and energy and pride, all of himself, poured it into this apartment for three years now, and look what had happened. His home, his home.

What would Matt say? Matt wouldn't really care, would he? Not really, not deeply, not the way Brock cared. Matt had never been all that interested in the apartment, in the plans for it. "You do it, baby," he'd say, grinning that grin of his, and pat Brock on the cheek and talk about something else instead.

He was alone with his grief. His rage. Grief and rage. There was no one on earth who would really, truly sympathize, understand, share this horrible experience with him. Never before in his life had he realized just how totally, miserably, incurably alone he really was.

The phone rang.

Startled, he looked at his watch, and it was five o'clock. Had he been here half an hour already? He'd come in, he'd seen the living room, he'd wandered like a zombie through the rest of the apartment, stunned and dazed by it all, and had finished in the living room again, his mind just refusing to comprehend what had happened. And then he'd fallen to the floor; he'd been sitting here like that ever since.

And here it was five o'clock already, and the phone was ringing.

It was on the floor now, over to his right. The upper air just seemed too high, too far up toward the ceiling, the top of the room; he couldn't get all the way up there, stand all the way up there. He got to hands and knees and crawled across the carpet to the phone and sat down again beside it. He picked up the receiver and in a strengthless, hopeless voice said, "Yes?"

"Paul?" It was Matt's voice, strong and confident.

"Yes."

"What's the matter? Something wrong there?"

"Oh, Matt." Brock shuddered and felt for a second as though he couldn't go on, he couldn't tell any more, he didn't have the strength to hold the phone anymore.

"What the hell's wrong?"

He took a deep breath. "He was here, Matt."

"Who, Parker? You saw him?"

"No. It was before — Matt, he wrecked the apartment!"

"He did what?"

"It's all — it's all —" Brock gestured wildly at the wreckage around him, as though Matt could see his waving arm and strained face. "He just — *killed* it, Matt. Everything broken, everything —"

"What did he find?" Matt's voice snapped through his own wailing.

"Find? I don't know what he found. What do you mean, find?"

"Did he get the guns? Did he get the money? Did he get the serum? Didn't you look around?"

"Matt, I didn't even —"

"*Look,* dummy! Get off your ass and look!"

"Matt, how could I be expec—"

"Look *now!*"

"All right," he said. "All right. I'll be right back. Matt?"

"What?"

"I wasn't sure you were still there. I'll be right back." He put the phone down and labored to his feet, as stiff and clumsy as a washerwoman. He went through the apartment, not looking at the destruction this time, looking for the signs of robbery, and he found them. He went back to the phone, turning a chair back onto its legs and sitting on its slit-open seat, picking up the receiver from the floor and saying into it, "Everything, Matt. He got everything."

Matt cursed. Angry, harsh words, clipped and bitter. Brock rubbed the heel of his free hand against his forehead, listening to the tinny words in his ear.

Finally Matt took a deep dreath and said, "Okay. He's number two on the list. We'll get him, baby, don't you worry."

"I want to kill him," Brock said in the same faint voice. "I want to do it myself, Matt."

"He's yours. But right now there's still number one. Uhl, he's the one we're after first."

Brock forced himself to ask, "Have you found him?" Though he didn't really care. He would never say anything to Matt, but he was thinking that none of this would have happened if Matt hadn't insisted on horning in between Parker and Uhl.

Matt said, "Sure I found him, baby, what do you think? I found out his drop, anyway, and that's all that matters. He's either there or he'll show up there. I'm gonna need you."

"All right."

"You don't want to stick around there anyway."

Brock looked at the room. "No. I don't."

"I'll meet you in Philly. I looked it up; there's a six-ten

104

express train gets in at seven forty-five. I'll meet you there."

"All right."

"Don't worry, baby. We'll have Uhl and the dough out of the way by tonight, and then we'll go settle the score with Parker."

"All right."

"And we can use a chunk of that thirty-three grand from Uhl," Matt said, "to put the apartment back in shape again. What do you think of that, huh?"

Voice dull, Brock said, "That will be fine, Matt." Thinking how very alone he was, that the only man in the world he was close to could be so ignorant about him. That Matt could think for a minute he would ever want to set foot in this apartment again. That Matt couldn't understand how it had been spoiled for him, that no amount of money on earth could make this apartment a virgin again. "I'll see you in Philadelphia, Matt," he said.

Four

Pam Saugherty said, "Well, I hope he never comes back at all."

Ed Saugherty said, "Frankly, I hope the same thing. Just to get you off my back about him."

"Is that any way to talk to me in front of the children?" Who were sitting with them at the dinner table, eyes round, ears open, mouths full of unchewed food.

Ed Saugherty knew there was no way to win an argument when his wife began hitting him in the head with the kids, so he just made a face and picked up his knife and fork and started cutting his roast beef.

Pam, having reduced him to silence, continued her half of the argument as a monologue, but he didn't really listen. He thought about George Uhl instead, and about his earnest prayer that George *wouldn't* come back. Not ever. Not at all.

And not just because of Pam either, though God knew that was a big part of it. But George was mixed up in something bad, and the longer George hung around here the greater the danger Ed Saugherty was going to get mixed up in it with him, and that was the last thing Ed wanted.

It wasn't like high school anymore. The world was different now; the responsibilities were different. Only George didn't seem to understand that. Back in high school he'd been an exciting guy to know, a risky, dangerous guy who drove cars too fast, drank before he was of legal age, got into fights with strangers, was always in trouble with the teachers at school; and it was fun to be a pal of his then, to share even just slightly in the excitement of his adventures. But when you're a kid nothing is for real, nothing counts, there aren't any responsibilities. That was what George failed to understand — that when a man grows up he has to set aside the things of a child, goddammit.

He remembered calling George four years ago, when he'd been up in New York with the convention, and he remembered with embarrassment how he'd deferred to George both evenings. In adult, practical, realistic terms it was Ed Saugherty who was on top of the heap and George Uhl who was on the bottom, but it hadn't worked out that way, and Ed knew it was his own fault. He'd still seen George as romantic and dramatic; he'd seen himself as a dull, plodding, uninteresting sort of guy, and he knew he'd spent those two evenings trying to win some sort of approval from George, approval and understanding. He'd even tried to buy his approval with that forty bucks they'd both known was a gift and not a loan.

At least he hadn't talked to George about women. That had been during the bad time with Pam. He'd come to New York determined to break his marriage vows, and when he'd called George it had been mainly in hopes George could arrange a double date or something, could line him up with a girl. But he hadn't been able to bring himself to ask the question, and George hadn't volunteered any such thing. Afterwards he'd been glad he hadn't embarrassed and humiliated himself at least that much. He'd done so enough as it was. With the forty bucks, and deferring to the man.

And the same thing Monday, four days ago, when George showed up in the dusty car, unshaved, a wild look in his eyes, full of desperate secrets, asking to be hidden out for a while. Ed had fallen immediately into the old attitudes towards George, admiring his derring-do, deferring to him, taking the subordinate position to him. And maybe this time it would wind up costing him more than forty bucks.

If George came back. But of course he'd come back; he'd left a suitcase in the closet in the guest room. And in his note he'd said he'd be back. But if only he wouldn't.

In a funny way, if it weren't for Pam he felt he could throw George out now. If he came back. Tell him, "I'm sorry, George, but I've got responsibilities to my family and I'm afraid you could wind up bringing them trouble, so I'm going to ask you to find somebody else to help you. I'm sorry, but that's the way it is." He could say that and mean it and know it was the best thing under the circumstances. Except for Pam. She'd turned it into a contest by now, a battle of wills, trying to force him around to her way of thinking, and of course that made it all impossible. To throw George out now would not be the way of reason, it would be giving in to Pam. Letting her win.

If there was only some way to get that fact across to her, to make her understand that if she'd only lay off she'd get what she wanted. But looking across the table now at her talking face he knew there wasn't a damn thing he was going to be able to do to change anything. Circumstances were rolling along, rolling along, and he was just swept up in it, and all he could do was hope for the best.

The phone rang.

It startled him and he dropped his knife, and that startled Pam, who stared at him in surprise a second and then said, "I'll get it."

He nodded and picked up the knife again. He watched her trim figure as she walked into the living room, thinking that George had no idea what he'd cost Ed already. He looked around the table, told Angela to chew her food, and then Pam came back and said, "It's for you. I think it's him."

"Oh." He got to his feet as she, cold-faced, sat down. He went into the living room and said hello into the telephone.

George. "Ed, we've got a problem." Sounding out of breath, rushed, harried.

Ed felt dinner lumping in his stomach. "A problem? What do you mean, a problem?"

"I'm not coming back there," George said, and Ed smiled at the phone. But then George said, "There's been a mess down here. I'm in Washington. There's a girl here" — his voice receded a bit as though he turned away from the phone to look at something for the next few words — "she's been beat up pretty bad. I got to take care of her, do something for her; then I'm getting out of here. I don't know where I'm going, but I'll get in touch."

"That's all right, George, you —"

"The big thing is the suitcase I left there," George said quickly. "You stash that someplace safe, you hear me?"

"Yes. I —"

"Don't tell your wife where. Just you do it by yourself."

Ed stiffened a little at that. "Pam wouldn't—"

"That isn't the question," George said. "The question is, it's better she doesn't know anything. Better for her. There's a guy might come around."

"What?"

"Ed, don't worry about it. Here's what you tell him."

"What do you mean, somebody might come around?"

"This girl here had to give him your phone number. He really leaned on her, Ed, he made a mess out of her. But all you do—"

"My phone number? George, what have you done to me?"

"Listen to me, goddammit. If he comes around, *if* he comes around, you tell him you used to know me when. I called you on the phone, I asked you to relay messages, you said okay. You got two messages, one yesterday, one today. The one yesterday was from a Matt Ros—"

"George, I can't—"

"Listen, Ed, you want him leaning on you too?"

"What is he after, George, the suitcase?"

"Hell, no! He's after me, Ed, what do you think? Listen, all you have to do is remember the two messages. You got them, I called you a while later, and you gave them to me, that's all you know. You don't know where I am or anything else. You got it?"

Pam had come to the doorway, napkin in hand. She was looking at him.

Ed said, "Are you sure I shouldn't call the police, George?"

"Ed, you've got an aiding a fugitive rap if you do. Now just listen to me."

"Aiding a —" Then he saw Pam in the doorway and stopped himself.

109

George was saying, "You don't have anything to worry about, Ed. He might not come around at all. Just stash the suitcase somewhere safe, and if this guy comes around give him the story. Two messages, and I called you both times. He's got no reason to call you a liar, so he'll go away. Right? Ed, you there?"

"I'm here." Ed licked his lips, watched his wife watching him in the doorway.

"I'll go over the messages with you," George said, and went over them with him. The names, the times the messages came, the phone number on the first message, the times George allegedly phoned him to get the messages. He made Ed repeat them, which he did, Pam frowning at him, and then George said, "I'll get in touch in a couple days. Now I got to get out of here. Don't worry about a thing, Ed." And hung up.

Ed kept holding the receiver to his ear. He knew George had hung up. He knew sooner or later he was going to have to hang up too, but until he did, until he broke the connection at his end, nothing could move forward. As soon as he hung up, reality would break in, Pam would start asking questions, strangers would come to the door. But not till he hung up the telephone.

He stood holding the receiver to his ear.

Five

Midnight. Matt Rosenstein stepped into the sidewalk phone booth and shut the door to make the light come on. He dialed the number, then opened the door partway again, enough to switch the light back off. Then he leaned against the glass wall and listened to the ringing.

Matt Rosenstein was a heavyset man of forty-two with irritable, intelligent eyes and a heavy, stupid jaw. He'd started pushing garment racks around Seventh Avenue in New York in his late teens, and the first crime for money he ever committed was helping punch some people out in an office down on Varrick Street. He never knew what it was all about and he never much cared. He and three other guys got thirty bucks each to go downtown and punch these people out, and they did, and that was it. And it was easier work than pushing garment racks up and down the sidewalk. In the twenty-four years since that incident, Rosenstein had committed most of the felonies on the books — kidnapping was about the only major exception — and every commission had been strictly for money. He'd burned people's diners down when they wanted a fire for the insurance. He'd stolen, he'd hijacked, he'd extorted, he'd blackmailed, he'd murdered, he'd swindled. Whatever came along, it never mattered. Money was money, and more money was more money, and a tough, thick-skinned guy with intelligent eyes and a stupid jaw could make out in this world.

Until four years ago when he'd met Paul Brock, his personal life had been bare but heterosexual. He'd taken sex the way he'd taken money, where he could get it and any way he could get his hands on it. It had never pleased him as much as money, but it had never occurred to him there might be any reason for that other than his own preoccupation or the dullness of the pigs he

111

invariably wound up with.

Paul Brock was a partner in a men's boutique on Hudson Street that needed a fire preceded by a robbery, and one of the other partners got onto Matt, and that was how they met. Matt looked at Brock, recorded the fact that he was a faggot, and ignored it. Business was business. But the night before the fire they were alone together in the stockroom, Brock explaining what to take and what to leave, and Matt found himself patting his cupped hand against the back of Brock's neck. Brock looked at him, and Matt saw the fear in Brock's eyes, and he shook his head and just kept patting. And Brock sort of went limp, his shoulders sagged and his eyes closed, and he leaned forward toward Matt as though he'd fallen over on his face, and that was how it started.

As far as Matt Rosenstein was concerned, though, he himself was still straight. Brock was a faggot, and the relationship they had was sex-based, but that was just because living with a guy had business advantages and other advantages over living with a broad. Matt was still straight, and when he got a shot at a woman he still took it and it still wasn't very good, but he was still straight.

Like Uhl's woman down in Washington this afternoon. Now, she might have been okay. She looked as though she ought to be a real tiger in the rack, but of course by the time she opened her head about Georgy Porgy she wasn't feeling too frisky anymore, and the way it turned out she lay there and took it when he climbed abroad. So it was fun, but not a hell of a lot fun. Anybody in his right mind would prefer a Paul Brock to something like that. You wouldn't have to be a fag.

And Paul came in handy in a lot of ways. Like at the moment he was on watch in front of the house. The two of them had been there since about eight o'clock this evening, waiting to see something happen, and nothing had happened. At twenty to twelve the last light went out in there, and that was when Matt said, "Stay here. If he comes out, let him have it in the leg. I'll be right back." And he'd driven here, to this phone booth on a corner three blocks away, and now the phone was making its ringing sound in his ear, and after fourteen rings there was at last a click, and then a silence, and than a shaky, small male voice said, "Hello?"

"Let me talk to George," Matt said.

There was a sharp intake of breath, and then silence, and then words in a rush: "There isn't any George here. You've got the wrong number."

"No, I don't, honey. I want to talk to George Uhl."

"There's no one here by that name." The voice was shakier than ever.

Had something got George's wind up? Had he taken off someplace? Matt said, "Then how do I get in touch with him?"

"I don't know. I don't know any George Uhl." The shakiness in his voice called him a liar with every word he said.

Matt nodded comfortably at the phone. "I'm okay, baby," he said. "I'm straight. I'm Matt Rosenstein. I just talked to George yesterday. I want to talk to him again, that's all."

"Matt Rosenstein?" The voice sounded uncertain now.

Matt frowned. Had it been a mistake to mention his name? George would be running from that guy Parker these days, wouldn't he? Not from Matt Rosenstein. He said, "Sure. George and me are old buddies."

Still uncertain, the voice said, "He mentioned your name. He did mention your name."

"Well, sure."

"But he isn't here now. I honestly don't know where he is." Then, with gathering certainty, "But if you want to leave a message—"

"When did he leave?"

"He never was here," the voice said very quickly again, and Matt knew he was lying. He'd just said he isn't here *now*. "But he'll be calling here," the voice said. "You want me to give him a message?"

"Sure," Matt said. "Tell him I called, will you?"

"Is there any place he can call you back? The same number as before?"

For a second Matt felt doubt. If this guy knew the number from the last message maybe he really was just another stage in the chain. Maybe messages went first to the broad in Washington and then after that up to this guy in Philadelphia and then to George himself anywhere in the country. Anywhere in the country. Just call his buddy in Philly every once in a while, see if there's any messages. George just might be that smart.

Except that this guy was too shaky, and his words contradicted each other, and Matt just had a feeling. George had been hid out here, right here, right in this guy's house. Maybe something had spooked him, maybe Parker was on the prowl again, or maybe the broad had got herself untied and to a phone — though he doubted that — and so George wasn't here anymore, but he had been here, and of that Matt was dead certain.

And George would want to keep in touch. He'd want a line into his regular life; he'd want to know how things were going. And he'd keep on doing it through this Ed Saugherty, it only stood to reason.

Matt said, "No, that number isn't good anymore. Just tell him I'll get in touch. Okay?"

"All right," the voice said.

"Bye," said Matt, his voice soft, and put the phone back on its hook. He nodded at the phone, thinking, and then went out and got into his car and drove back to where Paul was sitting next to a hedge on the front lawn across the street from the Saugherty house. Matt parked the car and got out and Paul came over and Matt asked him, "Anything happen?"

"A light went on is all. It's still on."

Matt look across the street, and a light was shining in the house somewhere. "I guess I got him nervous," Matt said. "Come on."

"Is he in there?"

Matt led the way across the street. "Not now. I don't think so,

114

not now. But he was. And Saugherty know where he went. Come on."

They didn't go direct to the front door but angled over to a corner of the house. Matt boosted Paul up and Paul stood on his shoulders, bracing himself with one hand against the wall while he reached up with a pair of wire cutters in the other and snipped the telephone wire. Then he got down to the ground again and they walked half a dozen steps to the garage door. Matt tried it and it lifted. They went in and Matt switched on the light and they shut the door again. They made no effort to be quiet.

The door between the garage and the kitchen was locked, but it had glass in the upper half. Matt took a pistol from under his jacket and smashed the glass with the butt. He reached through and unlocked the door and he and Paul stepped through. The kitchen was half lit with spill from the living room. They went into the house and shut the door behind them, and in the kitchen they met a wild-eyed man in bathrobe and pajamas and slippers, scuffing hurriedly across the floor in their direction. He stopped when he saw them and said, "What are you doing? What are you doing here?" It was the same voice Matt had heard on the phone.

Matt saw a light switch and clicked it on. Ed Saugherty squinted in the white glare, and Matt said to Paul, "Go check out the rest of the house."

"Just a minute," Saugherty said. "Just a minute." He made as though to block Paul's path, but Matt held the pistol up where Saugherty could see it, and Saugherty stayed where he was. Paul left the room.

They waited, neither saying anything. After a couple of minutes they heard a complaining woman's voice and then a kid crying because he didn't want to be awake. Saugherty said, "You can't just —" and then quit. Because they both knew Matt could. Just.

Paul called from the living room, "Okay, Matt."

Matt waved the pistol at Saugherty. "Let's join them."

They went into the living room. Paul had closed the drapes over the picture window. A woman looking angry and scared was sitting on the sofa with three kids lined out beside her. The kids all looked teary and scared.

Matt said to Paul, "This it?"

Paul said, "There's somebody been using the guest room, but he's gone now. No luggage or anything."

"So he isn't coming back," Matt said. "Or maybe he is."

The woman snapped, "He isn't. We didn't want him here, and we don't want you here."

Saugherty tried to shush her by patting the air with his hands, saying, "Pam. Pam."

"You make me sick," she told him and then didn't look at him anymore. She glared at Matt instead.

Matt said to Saugherty, "I'm the fella just phoned a little while ago."

"Rosenstein?"

"That's right. Very good. Matt Rosenstein. Now, all I want is to have a nice talk with George. You know? I'm sorry to get everybody out of bed this way, but I feel it's kind of urgent. So all you have to do is say where George went, and we'll go right away again."

Saugherty shook his head. "I don't know where he went. I really don't."

"That would be an awful shame," Matt said, "because we don't plan to leave here until we find out where he went. So if you really don't know, it isn't going to be so good for you."

"He's supposed to call," Saugherty said. He sounded desperate. He kept blinking. He said, "He told me he'd call, but he didn't tell me where he was or where he was going. I swear he didn't. But he'll call."

"Well, that's another shame," Matt said, "since we just cut the phone wires. So we're stuck with you telling us where George is. You see how it is?"

"But I don't *know!*"

"Well, then, maybe he'll come back," Matt said, and by the

expression that flicked across Saugherty's face for just a second he knew he'd hit on it. Saugherty's eyes glanced to one side, his mouth made a small grimace, and then it was over. But that was all Matt needed. He nodded and said, "Yeah, that'd be nice. He'll come back here. How soon do you figure he'll be back, Ed?"

Saugherty said, "He isn't coming back. He'll just call. When there's no answer, he'll be afraid to come back."

"Naw. Not if the phone's just out of order. He'll be back. And we'll just wait for him. Unless you've got some idea where he is? Some small idea?"

"I don't. I swear I don't."

The woman said, "Ed, if you're protecting that man —"

"For the love of God, Pam, do you think I'd —"

Matt turned to her, smiling his little smile. "Maybe *you* know something you'd like to tell us."

"*I* didn't talk to him," she snapped. "My husband talked to him when he called."

"He called?" Matt turned back to the husband. "When was this, Ed?"

"This afternoon."

"And what did he say, Ed?"

"He said he wasn't coming back, but he'd call, he'd let me know what was happening."

"He didn't say where he was?"

"He said he was in Washington; some girl was beaten up down there or something."

"In Washington."

"But he wasn't staying there. He said he was leaving right after the phone call."

"It's a mobile age," Matt said. "It's easy to forget that. So the son of a bitch was in Washington today, was he?" He looked at Paul. "He'll be back, won't he?"

"I don't know, Matt. The phone out of order could scare him off."

"Can you splice it, patch it up?"

117

"Maybe. It looked like there was some tools and stuff out in the garage."

Matt thought and then nodded. "Okay. We'll fix the phone and we'll wait. And George will call, and Ed, you'll tell him everything's okay here, he can come back, no trouble. And you better sound convincing."

"Oh, I will," Saugherty said, and all at once he sounded bitter. "I don't owe George Uhl anything, don't you worry."

"I'm not worried," Matt said.

Paul said, "You want me to fix the phone now, Matt?"

"Not yet. A little later. Right now you keep an eye on everybody while the little lady gives me a tour of the house." He smiled at her and saw the startled expression on her face. But she wasn't as tough as that bitch down in Washington this afternoon; she wouldn't take as much convincing. There'd be a lot of energy left in her when they got to it.

Paul said, "Must you?" His voice was full of hurt, like always.

Matt shrugged, grinning at him. "Just a boyish peccadillo," he said. "It don't mean anything, baby." He turned and took a step over to the wife. He put his hand out. "Come on, Pam, I got the hots to see your house."

"Don't touch me," she said and leaned back against the sofa to keep away from him.

He leaned forward to take her arm, and she slapped at his hand, and he slapped her hard across the face. One of the kids let out a shriek.

Saugherty shouted something and ran at Matt. Everybody always needed convincing. He reached out one hand and held Saugherty with it and used the other hand to start hitting him.

Six

The doorbell woke Joyce Langer from a dream in which seven old crones who smelled like bacon were trying to drown her beside a rowboat on a cold, black river surrounded by fog. She came out of the dream slowly, almost reluctantly, fighting off the bony hands for a long time, her mind confused in its attempt to fit the sound of the ringing into her dream somehow, a black stone church with a bell ringing in its steeple appearing out of the fog just as the fog crumbled away entirely and she was awake, in bed, in a room in a building on West 87th Street in New York City, alone, unhappy, in darkness, with the doorbell ringing.

Her clock radio over on the dresser had a luminous dial, and it read twelve minutes past one o'clock in the morning. Who would be ringing her bell at a time like this?

She thought of Tom Lynch, the strange tough man who'd taken her to dinner this evening. Could he be back? She had a sudden sexual vision, almost physically staggering in its effect, and then it drained away again and she admitted to herself just how unlikely it was that Tom Lynch would have returned at this hour, and how much more remote from possibility that he would be here to have sex with her. She knew the kind of man she attracted, the kind of man she could succeed with, and he wasn't it.

Then who was it? The doorbell rang again as she switched on the light and got out of bed, smoothing her peach pajamas down over her legs. Various people from the past flickered through her mind as she went to the closet for her robe, and then she thought of George Uhl, and she stopped with the robe half on, knowing that that was who it was.

George Uhl.

She was suddenly terrified. She'd never been afraid of George before, not really afraid, but what she was feeling now was terror, and she quickly analyzed it for what it was. Guilt. Guilt at having helped Tom Lynch, George's enemy.

Had George found out? Was he coming to get even with her?

Paranoia lies close beneath every skin. She wondered briefly if Tom Lynch had been a trick, a test set up by George to see if he could trust her. Then Lynch had gone back to him and said, "She spilled everything about you, George." Now George was here to pay her back.

The thumb out there jabbed and jabbed at the bell. She couldn't ignore it, no matter what.

She ran through the apartment, her throat constricted as though she were wearing a too-tight necklace. She stopped at the door, breathless, panting as though she'd run a mile, and stooped to peer through the peephole in the door, seeing the face there she'd known she would see.

But not the expression. Not anger, not cold rage, not the determination to get even with anybody. As she watched, he turned his head and looked over his shoulder, and she saw how loosely his jaw hung. He turned back this way to ring the bell again, and she saw how pale the skin was around his eyes, how large his eyes looked.

He was terrified. *George* was terrified.

Now guilt wrapped her completely. She'd betrayed George to Tom Lynch, and the result was now outside her door, frightened, urgent, desperate. Coming to her for protection.

She unlocked the door and opened it, and George burst in, shoving the door so that it smacked painfully into her shoulder. "Took long enough," he said and slammed the door again.

The only light was the pale line across the floor from the ceiling light in the bedroom. She stood there, unable to think, and he switched on the nearest floor lamp and looked at her. "Still the same," he snapped as though it were an accusation. He jerked his head at the bedroom. "You got anybody in there?"

120

She shook her head. She couldn't think.

"Not you," he said. His own fear had made him scornful and savage. He turned away from her and strode off toward the bedroom.

She trailed after him, trying to sort out the moods in her head. She got to the bedroom and saw him standing beside the bed, leaning one hand on the wall while he kicked his shoes off. He looked over at her and said, "I'm in a jam. I need to be hidden out for a while."

She nodded, looking at him wide-eyed.

He made an obvious mammoth attempt to be agreeable to her, sticking a false smile on his face and saying, "You're the only one I can trust, Joyce. It's always you I come to when I'm in trouble."

A dull anger, like the beginning of heartburn, began inside her. It was such a cheap and obvious lie. He didn't even work very hard to make her believe it. She was supposed to be grateful for whatever dregs she got; she wasn't supposed to look the gift horse in the mouth. All he had to do was give her the bare outline of the role she was to play, and then she would play it.

Had it always been that way? The anger turned sour because it had.

He was taking off his shirt. "You don't know how it's been, Joyce," he was saying. "On the run like this." He came walking over to her, that smile on his face. "You were the only one I could turn to."

She knew it was a lie. She knew it was a lie. She stood there and let him put his arms around her, her body shivering inside the blue robe and the peach pajamas. In the last instant before his face was too close to be in focus she saw the expression change on it, saw it turn scornful and sure of itself. But then he was kissing her, his hands were stroking the bathrobe, and there was nothing to do but close her eyes and not believe or remember what she'd seen or what she knew, close her eyes and put her arms around him and believe whatever she wanted to believe.

His one hand slid down her back, down past the indentation of her waist, down over the curve of her rump, cupping against the bottom of her torso, pulling her close against his body. She felt him against her, and she felt how hungry she was, and she stopped agonizing over it. Even when he murmured her name in her ear, giving her a spurious individuality, she ignored what she knew.

Desire was completely physical and impersonal on both sides, and concentrated that way it made them clumsy with haste. Clothing was in the way, cumbersome and difficult to remove. Their arms were full of elbows, getting in their way. They fell over onto the bed, lying diagonally across it, all wrong, legs hanging out in mid-air from knees down.

She squeezed her eyes shut, and she was very noisy.

In the calm after the storm she opened her eyes and looked up and he was grinning at her. "You're okay, Joyce," he said, and she knew it was the first thing he'd actually said to *her* since coming in here. She smiled bashfully and reached up to touch his chest.

He lifted away from her, looking somewhere else. Kneeling beside her he stretched and yawned and scratched his chest and said, "Boy, I'm beat. You still working up at the college?"

Three words, that was all she was going to get. The moment was past already. She said "Yes."

"Don't wake me, okay? I had a rough day." He crawled over her as though she were a bunched-up blanket and lay down with his head on the pillow. "You wouldn't believe the kind of day I had," he said, he eyes closing. "Would you believe I drove from Philadelphia to Alexandria, Virginia, and from there to Washington, and from there to here? All in one day?"

"That's a lot of driving," she said and sat up. She wanted to cry, but she wasn't going to.

"You're damn right," he said. He pulled the covers up over himself. "See you tomorrow," he said, and rolled over on his side so that when she got into bed next to him his back would be to her.

She looked at his shoulder covered by blanket. She didn't think about tonight at all; she thought about the past. Other times with George. Things he'd done, things he'd said, things he'd failed to do. And other men, all of them like George one way or another. Things they'd done. Things they'd said. Things they'd failed.

She got to her feet. He was asleep already. She picked up her pajamas from the floor, and the waist button on the pajama bottoms had been pulled off. She bit the inside of her cheek because she wasn't going to cry. She dropped the pajamas on the floor again, picked up the robe instead, put it on, left the room, shut the door quietly behind her.

The white pages phone book was under the telephone in the living room. She sat on the sofa, her chin trembling, and looked up the number, then dialed it. She listened to the ringing sound, wondering if she would hang up when it was answered.

"Rilington Hotel."

"Oh," she said. "Uh."

"Yes?"

She hunched over the phone, her voice low but steady. "I want to leave a message for Mr. Thomas Lynch," she said.

FOUR

One

The mirror reflected Parker's pencil flashlight. He stood inside the door he'd just jimmied and moved the flashlight and saw that the mirror ran the length of the room and all the way up the wall, maybe twelve feet high. A huge mirror facing a bare, wood-floored room. A piano in a far corner of the room, a piano far away in a room corner in the mirror. Portable phonographs on wooden tables, real and image. A few chairs along the wall opposite the mirror facing the chairs far away against the back wall inside the mirror.

The door was closed as far as it would go. Parker moved away from it, crossing the room in front of the mirror, ignoring the distracting image of himself and the echo of the flashlight next to him. He came to a curtained doorway and clicked off the light and then carefully moved the curtain an inch out of the way.

Darkness. No light anywhere, no sound anywhere. He stepped through, the curtain brushing against him, smelling dusty, and when the curtain had fallen into place behind him again he hit the flashlight button briefly, just long enough to see where he was.

A living room, small and crowded, full of spindly-looking Danish modern. An archway opposite, with a small dining room beyond it.

There was no obstruction between here and the dining room. Parker moved slowly through the blackness, and when he thought he was to the archway he flicked on the light again.

Formica-topped dining room table in a wood grain effect. Six chairs with red seats. Sideboard on the right, windows on the left. Left side of the opposite wall a doorway to what looked like a hall.

He turned left in darkness, moved to the wall, traveled along it. When he felt the glass of the first window he stopped and tried to look out, but the blackness outside was unbroken. An air shaft, probably. He moved on and reached the doorway. He stopped and flicked the light again.

A hallway, fairly long, with linoleum flooring. Two doorways on the right, both doors open, a bathroom visible through the first, the second one too far away to see anything. What looked like a kitchen at the far end of the hall.

Darkness again. He moved down the hall, touching both walls till he came to the emptiness of the second doorway. He stood in that doorway and he could see the vague outlines of heavily draped windows across the way. He listened and heard nothing and flashed light again.

Somebody in bed.

In the after-image, when the light was out again, he frowned at what he'd seen. A woman in bed, asleep, covers up to her neck, lying on her back. But there was something wrong with it, something wrong with the picture.

He moved around the wall, around a chair, around a dresser, stopped when he knew he was near the bed. He listened.

No sound. No breathing. Nothing.

He leaned far over, straining in the darkness, listening.

Inhale. Very faint, very slow, very long. Exhale, the same. A pause, a long pause, and then another inhale and another exhale.

There was a bedside table right next to him, and when he reached out his hand he touched a lampshade. He reached under it, found the switch, turned the light on. He squinted down at the woman in the bed.

She'd been worked over. Twice, the second time by a doctor. There were bruises on her face and a bandage on her jaw under the right ear. Her left arm, lying on top of the covers, showed dark bruises on the forearm and the three middle fingers in splints.

There were bottles of pills and a glass of water on the bedside table. There was a recent puncture mark on her upper arm. Barri Dane was out and was going to stay out for a while.

127

Parker shook his head. He looked around the room and saw a chair across the way with some ripped and rumpled clothing on it. He went over and dumped the clothing on the floor and sat down facing the bed. He looked at the woman lying there and wondered what to do next.

His path had finally crossed Rosenstein's, that much was obvious. Had Barri Dane had anything to tell? If she had, Rosenstein already knew it, and it could be a couple of days before she could tell it to Parker. So what else was there to do?

It was well after midnight. He'd driven up and down the eastern seaboard all day today, starting with Grace Weiss in Wilkes-Barre this morning, then Lew Pearson in Alexandria, back north to Joyce Langer and Howie Progressi in New York, and now back south again to Washington. Almost twelve hours in the car, and nothing to show for it.

If only Uhl had gone to Progressi. Rosenstein hadn't tried that one, and Parker would have been clearly safely ahead of him. But Progressi hadn't know a thing.

Parker had made sure of that, though not as heavily as Rosenstein had done with Barri Dane. But Progressi was a loudmouth, a big talker with a belligerent facade, and that type never took long to empty. Just turn them upside down and everything they had spilled right out.

Parker had found him in the third place he looked, a bowling alley off Flatbush Avenue. He kept it calm and quiet at first, just telling Progressi he had a message for him from George Uhl.

Progress looked interested. "George? Something up?"

"Come on outside."

"I'm in the middle of a game, pal."

"You'll be back."

So Progressi shrugged and came out with him and they got into Parker's car and Parker hit him in the throat. Then he sat there and waited till Progressi could talk again, when he said, "I'm looking for George."

Progressi had a heavy face with a beard-blue jaw, but his skin was now white and unhealthy looking. Both hands were still up protectively around his throat, and when he spoke his voice was hoarse, "Whadaya hit *me* for?"

"So you'll tell me where I find George."

"You want his address? He's in the phone book, for Christ's sake. He's down in Washington in the phone book."

"You're gonna try my patience," Parker said, and backhanded him.

"Jesus!"

"All I want to know is how I find George."

"I dunno! I dunno!"

Parker hit him again.

"What's the matter with you? I don't know. He isn't home? I don't know where he is, I swear to Christ I don't."

Parker sat back. "Anybody else been asking about him?"

"About George? No. My nose is bleeding. You got any Kleenex? My nose is bleeding."

"No. Where am I going to find George?"

"Maybe his girl knows." Progressi was snuffling, putting his head back. His fingers and wrists were bloody from his nose.

Parker said, "What girl?"

"Down in Washington. Barri Dane, her name is. With an i. She'd know where he is. Christ, what's he done to you?"

"Maybe he'll tell you someday," Parker said. "You can go back to your game now."

Progressi didn't believe it. He blinked at Parker, blinked at the door handle. "I can go?"

"Put some ice on the back of your neck," Parker told him. "It stops the bleeding."

Progressi opened the car door. "You want to try this stuff on George," he said. His voice was shaky. "You can't push everybody around like this, not everybody."

Parker waited for him to get out of the car.

Progressi licked blood from his upper lip. He was blinking and blinking, trying to figure some way to get his assurance back. "I'll see you again sometime," he said, saying it less tough than he wanted.

Parker waited.

Progressi got out of the car and stood there with the door open a second. "You're a real son of a bitch," he said. "You're a goddam bastard, you know that?"

Parker started the engine and drove away from there, and the acceleration shut the passenger door. He drove straight down the coast to Washington and here was his first sign of Matt Rosenstein, and Barri Dane wasn't going to be answering anybody's questions for quite a while.

He shifted in the chair, looking across the room at her. If she'd wake up. But she wasn't going to, she'd been doped to the ears. It would be tomorrow sometime before she opened her eyes at all, and she'd still be groggy then.

And he didn't even know for sure she had anything to tell. It looked as though Rosenstein had worked on her a long time, maybe for as long as she'd stay conscious for it, so it could be she didn't know anything at all and Rosenstein had just been tough to convince.

Why hadn't Rosenstein brought along that drug of his? Maybe he preferred to ask his questions this way, if it was a woman.

But the hell with Rosenstein. The question was, What was Parker going to do now? There was nothing left except the cop in New York, Dumek, the one Joyce Langer had told him about. A patrolman named Dumek. He might be tough to find, and even if he was found he was a real long shot to know anything. Dumek might be one hundred percent crooked, he might be on the take every way there was, but he was still an unlikely guy for Uhl to go to with his hands full of caper money. But what the hell else was there?

He got to his feet, suddenly impatient. He wanted to go somewhere and there wasn't anywhere to go. All this driving today, up and down, back and forth, hour after hour, and he hadn't gotten anywhere at all. And he wanted to do more of it. His mind was full of the urge to get into the car and drive, just drive. Just to be doing something.

He remembered having seen a phone in the living room. He left the bedroom and went back through the flat, this time switching on lights as he went, and in the living room he dialed New York information for the number he wanted, then dialed it. Not out of any expectation, but just to be doing something.

"Rilington Hotel."

"Hello, this is Thomas Lynch. You have any messages for me?"

"One moment, sir."

He waited, sitting on the edge of the chair, free hand dangling between his knees. He was tired, but he knew he couldn't sleep. His shoulders ached; the back of his neck ached.

"Sir?"

"Yeah?"

"Are you registered with us?"

"Not at the moment."

"Well, we do have a message here, Mr. Lynch, but I have no record of your having made a reservation."

"I sent a wire. You've got a message for me?"

"I have no record of the wire, sir. But if you could give me the information now, I'd be happy to see to the arrangements."

There was a message there. He wasn't using that hotel for a drop with anybody but Joyce Langer. Sometimes the unexpected happens.

But he had the desk clerk's game to play first. He said, "I wanted a single for four days from Tuesday. What's the message?"

"That would be this coming Tuesday, sir?"

"Naturally. Now if you don't mind, it's late and I'm tired. What's the message?"

"Oh, I'm sorry. A Miss Langer called for you, not more than an hour ago. I didn't take the message myself. Let me see.... She said she has what you were looking for, and if you will come by between eight and eleven in the morning the superintendent will have the key for you. She will not herself be at home."

"Good," Parker said. His watch said nearly one o'clock. It

was four hours back to New York; that meant five. Four hours sleep, he could be up to her place by nine-thirty. He said, "That means a change in the reservation. I want it to start tonight."

"Tonight, sir?"

"I'll be there in four hours."

"That would be five in the morning, sir."

"I know that."

"We'd have to charge you the full rate for tonight, sir. I hope you understand that."

"I understand that," Parker said.

"Very well, sir. We'll be looking forward to serving you."

Parker hung up and went back to the bedroom. The woman hadn't moved. Her breathing was still slow and faint. He switched off the lamp beside the bed and then left the apartment, turning out lights as he went. He paid no attention to his reflection as he crossed the long studio to the jimmied door. He went out, closed the door behind him as far as it would go, went back to his car, and started to drive again.

Two

Parker poked George Uhl in the stomach with the barrel of the pistol. "Wake up," he said.

Uhl groaned and thrashed a little in the rumpled bed, not wanting to be awake. Then his eyes did open, unfocused, as though his sleeping brain was just starting to listen to the voice that had spoken to him, listen to it and identify it.

Uhl jolted up to a sitting position, wide-eyed. He'd been sleeping naked. He stared at Parker, and for a long minute neither of them said anything. Then Uhl said, "No."

Parker had backed away a few steps, and now he motioned with the gun, saying, "Get up out of there. Get dressed."

"What are you going to do?"

"Up," Parker said.

Uhl looked around as though just now noticing where he was. "That bitch," he said and showed a sudden flare-up of anger. "That little bitch, she turned me up."

"Don't let it worry you, George," Parker said. "Just get out of bed. Don't make me lose my patience."

Uhl glanced at him as though Parker were suddenly the secondary problem, as though he didn't want to be distracted from thinking about Joyce Langer. He said, "You don't have any patience to lose. You never had any patience." He threw the covers back and got out of bed.

Parker leaned against the wall and kept the gun pointed generally in Uhl's direction while Uhl dressed. Uhl was wrong about his not having any patience. He'd been impatient up till now, impatient since Uhl had turned the robbery sour Monday morning, just this time of the morning five days ago, but now that he had Uhl in front of him again he wasn't impatient at all. He was very relaxed, very calm, ready to take his time and do the rest of this right.

He'd gotten here fifteen minutes ago, at nine forty. The super had given him the key and he'd come up, let himself in quietly, found Uhl asleep in the bedroom, and proceeded to search the place. If Uhl was carrying the money with him, it was all over and Uhl would never wake up again.

But the apartment was clean. He hadn't been able to give it the kind of thorough frisk he'd given Paul Brock's place, but it didn't need it. That wad of money Uhl had taken off with was large and bulky, no matter what sort of container it was put in. If it had been anywhere in the apartment Parker would have found it in the ten minutes he'd spent looking. But it wasn't here, and that meant George Uhl got to greet one more morning.

They didn't say anything while Uhl dressed, but obviously he'd been thinking things over because once he was dressed he looked at Parker and said, "You want the dough or I'd be dead now."

"That's right."

"That means we can work out a deal."

"Maybe," Parker said.

Uhl shrugged. "Why not? If I'm dead you'll never get the money. If I don't give you the money I'm dead. So why can't we work out a deal? Should be the simplest thing in the world. You had breakfast?"

Uhl was being calm too, showing casual, unruffled, untroubled surface, and that had to mean he was waiting to see where his edge was coming from. Parker told him, "Don't think about breakfast, think about the money you took. Where is it?"

Uhl shook his head. "Uh-uh. It isn't going to work that way, Parker. I tell you now where to find it, and what happens? You go bang and you walk out of here and go get the cash, and I'm not breathing anymore. I said a deal, Parker, and I meant a deal. I meant I'm going to buy my life from you, and the whole question is how much it's going to cost me." Uhl smiled with one side of his mouth. "I'm going to go on living, Parker," he said, "and that means I'm going to be needing breakfast. Don't

134

shoot me while I go through this doorway here."

Uhl started through the doorway and Parker stepped over quickly in front of him and slapped him across the face with the barrel of the gun. Uhl flipped over backwards onto the floor and Parker kicked him and then stood back and watched him again. He felt very patient, very measured. He had all the time in the world.

Uhl came up slowly. His cheek was bleeding, and his face finally looked frightened. His voice was a little shaky now too, but what he said was, "Parker, that way don't do it. You won't kick it out of me, you really won't, because I'll keep remembering that as soon as I tell you where the money is you'll stop kicking and start shooting. You won't get it that way, Parker, I swear you won't."

"You may be right," Parker said. He switched the gun to his left hand. "Get up," he said.

"Sure I'm right," Uhl said. A relieved smile flashed across his face. Starting awkwardly to his feet he said, "Just let me make myself some break—"

He was halfway up, bent forward. Parker swung from the floor and hit him across the jaw with his closed fist. Uhl jerked around in a half circle, his arms flopping out in front of him, and fell face down across the foot of the bed, his feet hanging back pigeon-toed on the floor.

Parker checked him and he was out. He dragged him all the way up onto the bed and rolled him over onto his back, then took from his jacket pocket the small bottle of serum he'd found at Brock's place and a hard-pack cigarette box, and shook out the hypodermic needle, now in its two parts. He screwed the parts together and put the hypo on the table beside the bottle.

He'd brought this along just in case, though he would have preferred not to use it. He wasn't one hundred per cent sure it was the same stuff that had been used on him, and he had no idea what the right dose was or what an overdose might do. But there'd been a good chance Uhl would react the way he had, and in that case there was the serum to fall back on.

He rolled Uhl's sleeve up, exposing his arm all the way to the shoulder. Judging from the small puncture mark in his own arm after the serum had been used on him, it was injected directly into the vein in the inner part of the elbow. Parker turned Uhl's limp arm on the sheet, saw the faint blue line beneath the skin, touched it with one finger. A slight ridge, almost too slight to feel. But if he could see it he could hit it.

He'd never worked with a hypodermic needle before, but he'd seen it done in the movies and on television, and a few times he'd watched doctors getting ready to give him a shot. He didn't have the usual interest in sterile precautions, so that simplified matters. He picked up the bottle and needle and studied them. If he had it figured right, he should depress the plunger all the way in the syringe, poke the needle through the cork in the top of the bottle, then gradually pull the plunger out again, filling the syringe with the fluid from the bottle. Then pull the needle out of the cork, stick it in Uhl's arms, and depress the plunger again. No. Squirt a little first, to be sure he wasn't injecting air in the vein, because that would kill Uhl before he could talk.

There was about two-thirds left in the bottle. Assuming he'd been the first one it had been used on, he should now take about half the remainder. He did, having no difficulty, and injected it slowly into Uhl's arm. The plunger resisted him, not wanting to shove the fluid into Uhl's vein quickly, and he just kept a slow and steady pressure on it and quit while there was still a trace of fluid in the syringe. Then he took the hypo apart again, put the parts back in the cigarette box, and tucked the box and bottle back into his pocket.

Uhl hadn't moved. Parker leaned over him and said, "George."

Nothing.

"George, wake up."

No reaction.

Parker slapped his face and called his name again. He tugged at Uhl's hair, slapped him harder. Still nothing.

So he'd have to wait. That was all right, he had time.
He went over to a chair and sat down.

Three

When the front door banged open, Parker got out of the chair fast and stepped behind the bedroom door. His pistol was in his hand, his back against the wall, his head turned so he could look through the crack between door and jamb and see whoever it was before they got all the way into the room.

But he heard her before he saw her. "George!" she cried, running through the apartment. "George, wake up!"

Joyce Langer.

There had always been the chance she'd change her mind, and she was the type to do it too late. Parker waited where he was.

She came running into the room and skidded to one knee beside the bed. "George!" she started to shake his shoulder. "George, you've got to wake up! There's a man after you! There's a man named Lynch after you!"

Parker shut the bedroom door. "He knows me under a different name," he said.

She spun so fast she almost lost her balance and fell over, grabbing Uhl's upper arm at the last second to help her keep her balance. "You!"

"You should have phoned," Parker told her. "You wouldn't be in trouble now."

"I couldn't tell him on the phone," she said. "What I did, I couldn't tell him what I did."

"Second guessers always make trouble for themselves," Parker said. "Get up from there."

She said, "Don't do anything to — I shouldn't have. Don't do anything to him because of what I did. Please." She turned and shook his arm again. "George, wake *up*!" Then she stared at him, struck finally by his lack of response, by the way he was

138

just lying there. "George? George?"

He could hear panic and hysteria building in her voice. He said, "He's alive. Don't worry about him, he's alive."

"What did you do to him? What in the name of God did you do to him?"

He walked closer to her. "You shouldn't have come back here."

She stared up at him. "What are you going to do? What am I involved in? What's going on?"

Uhl groaned, startling them both. Immediately she was all over him, tugging at his shoulders, shouting into his face: "George, George, wake up, *please* wake up!"

He mumbled something. His face was frowning, but other than that he still wasn't moving.

Parker took the girl by the arm. "Up out of there," he said. "You came at a bad time."

She didn't want to go. He had to tug harder. He knew she'd start screaming soon, and he couldn't have that. In any case, he couldn't have her in this room listening when he started asking his questions. He said, loud and commanding, "Joyce!"

She automatically turned her head to look up at him and he clipped her with a short, hard right hand. She bounced back against the edge of the bed and would have fallen to the floor if he hadn't held on to her.

She was out. He picked her up and carried her into the living room and dumped her on the sofa, then went back to the bedroom and went through dresser drawers and found stockings and belts and a clean handerchief. He took these back to the living room and bound and gagged her. She would keep now, for a while. But she still complicated things; her presence here still made the situation too difficult.

But he could work all that out later. He went back to the bedroom and Uhl had faded back down into sleep again, the frown lines gone from his face. Parker took the chair he'd been sitting in and pulled it over beside the bed and sat down. He already had a pencil and a piece of paper on the bedside table.

He said, "George."

A faint frown.

"George, listen to me. Wake up and listen to me."

The frown deepened; it became petulant, like a child not wanting to wake up from a nap. Uhl's head moved slowly back and forth, once to the left and once to the right, as though he wanted to shake his head in a *no* gesture but couldn't because it was too much effort.

"Wake up, George. Listen to me. Can you hear me? George? Can you hear me, George?"

He wasn't getting all the way through. He reached over and slapped Uhl's face, not hard, and Uhl said, "*Unn*-nn," the frown deepening even more into an exaggerated grimmace, the eyes squeezing shut as though a bright light had been aimed at them.

"George? Can you hear me?"

"Ohh," said Uhl, still grimacing, the sound petulant.

"Can you hear me?"

"Yes." As though to say leave me alone.

"This is Parker. Do you know who I am?"

"Yes." Said more calmly now, as though he was getting more resigned to answering questions.

"Who am I?"

"You're Parker."

"And who are you?"

"George. George Uhl."

"You took some money away from me."

No answer.

Parker looked at him, wondering if he'd faded out again, but then remembered his own session with this drug. It was necessary to phrase the sentences as direct questions, obviously requiring an answer. Statements weren't answered, only questions were answered.

All right. He said, "Do you remember taking some money away from me?"

"Yes." Very prompt, and without any emotional reaction at

140

all. Uhl's eyes were still closed but in a more relaxed way now, no longer squeezed shut. He seemed calm now, his answers calm, almost mechanical.

Parker said, "Where is that money? The money you took from me."

"I don't know."

That couldn't be the right answer. Was the drug not working? Had he given too little? He looked at Uhl's face, but he couldn't believe Uhl was acting. The drug was affecting him, it had to be. Then how could he come up with an answer like that?

Was it true? Had the damn fool managed to lose the money sometime in the last five days?

Parker said, "What did you do with the money?"

"Left it with Ed."

That was better. There was an explanation in here somewhere. All he had to do was work out the right questions to ask. He picked up the pencil and wrote *Ed* on the paper, then said, "Ed who?"

"Saugherty."

"Spell it. Will you spell that name?"

Uhl spelled it, slowly and steadily, like a talking computer, and Parker wrote it down.

Parker said, "You left the money with Ed Saugherty. What did Ed Saugherty do with the money?"

"Hid it."

"He hid it from you?"

Uhl frowned. The question was too complicated for him somehow.

Parker found another way to phrase it. "Did he hide the money *for* you?"

Uhl's expression cleared. He was contented again. He said. "Yes."

"Do you know where he hid it?"

"No."

"When did he hide it?"

"Friday."

That would be yesterday. Parker said, "Were you staying with Ed Saugherty before you came here?"

"Yes."

"Why did you leave there?"

"Matt Rosenstein was after me."

"How do you know?"

"He beat up Barri."

"Did you see Barri?"

"Yes."

"Did you call the doctor for her?"

"Yes."

Parker grimaced. He and Uhl had been doing a long-distance dance up and down the eastern seaboard for three days. He'd gotten to Pearson before Uhl, but Uhl had caught up. And then Uhl had gotten to Barri Dane before Parker, but Parker didn't catch up. But that was all right, because Parker had gotten to Joyce Langer before Uhl, and that meant everything was caught up.

But if only the timing had been a little different somewhere along the line.

Parker said, "Did Barri Dane tell Matt Rosenstein anything?"

"Phone number."

"What phone number?"

"Ed's phone number."

"Could Rosenstein get to Ed through that phone number?"

"Yes."

Which meant Rosenstein was now a full day ahead of him. Had he gotten the money away from this Ed Saugherty?

Parker said, "Where do you know Ed Saugherty from?"

"High school."

Parker frowned. It was another strange answer. He said, "What does Ed Saugherty do?"

"Works for a computer company."

"You mean he's legit?"

142

"Yes."

Another problem. It had been smart of Uhl to do that, pick somebody on the outside to hole up with, somebody that didn't have any connections to his bent life, but now that everything was blown open it made for complications. With Rosenstein and Parker both descending on him, this Ed Saugherty would probably be calling copper or anyway confusing the issue.

Parker said, "Where does Ed Saugherty live?"

"Philadelphia."

Another drive. Ninety miles this time. If it weren't such a time-consuming pain in the ass it would be comic.

Parker asked for the address and wrote down Uhl's answer. He then had Uhl describe the house, give physical descriptions of Saugherty and the other members of his family, and give a general description of the neighborhood.

A solid, middle-class family in a solid, middle-class development. All very straight, all very innocent, all having no idea how to handle the kind of situation they were in now. With Saugherty's wife already giving her husband static about Uhl, according to Uhl. What would she be doing with Rosenstein and Parker descending on the household?

In fact, with Rosenstein a day ahead of him, there was no telling what sort of situation existed down there now. The thing could have blown wide open to the cops. Rosenstein could have been in and gotten the money and gone away already. A lot could have happened. Parker could pick Uhl's brain clean and he'd still be going down there to a blind situation. He could be walking to a house full of law, or a house full of Rosenstein, or even a house where Ed Saugherty had grabbed himself a gun and gone on the alert. Anything could have happened; anything could happen next.

Parker next asked, "Who else knows about the money besides you and me and Rosenstein and Ed Saugherty?"

"Nobody."

"Not Barri Dane?"

"No."

143

"Not Joyce Langer?"

"No."

"You've been with Ed Saugherty, and Barri Dane, and Joyce Langer. You went to Lew Pearson's, when you shot him. Where else have you been?"

"Nowhere."

"Haven't you seen anybody else?"

"No."

All right. At least he now was sure of how many were in the game. The odds were still against him, but at least he knew how many were playing. He folded the piece of paper and put it away in his pocket. Then he got to his feet and left the bedroom.

The phone was in the living room, beside the sofa. Joyce Langer was still unconscious. Parker sat down near her feet and dialed the Philadelphia number he'd gotten from Uhl.

It was answered on the second ring by a noncommital voice that asked, "Hello?"

"Ed Saugherty?"

"Speaking," said the voice. It was vaguely reminiscent.

"I'm calling for George," Parker said. "You know who I mean?"

"Of course," said the voice. "Where is George?"

"He thinks it would be safer for you if you didn't know," Parker said. "But he wants the money. You know, the suitcase?"

"The suitcase? Oh. Yes, the suitcase." But the voice seemed doubtful. And it was reminding Parker of something or somebody.

"He wants you to bring it up to New York," Parker said.

"Sure," said the voice. "Where is it?"

It wasn't Saugherty. Saugherty knew where the money was; Saugherty was the only one on earth who knew where the money was. This wasn't Saguherty.

Then Parker recognized the voice at last, and without saying anything more he hung up and headed for the bedroom.

The voice had been Paul Brock's.

Four

Uhl was lying there like the body at a wake, his face expressionless. Parker stood beside the bed and said, "Can you open your eyes?"

In a faraway voice Uhl said, "I don't know."

"Try."

Uhl's eyelids raised. His eyes looked up toward the ceiling, but they didn't seem to be focused on anything.

"Try sitting up," Parker said.

Uhl seemed very uncoordinated. He moved clumsily, his arms and legs beating ineffectively as he tried to get up off his back. Parker finally had to help him, but once he was sitting up he could stay there on his own, though he tilted a bit to one side. His arms hung down and his eyes were still looking straight ahead, still unfocused.

Parker got him on his feet. He was very weak, though willing to do whatever he was told to do. With Parker helping to support him, they walked out of the bedroom and through the apartment.

The problem was, he couldn't leave Uhl here because he didn't know how long it would take for the drug to wear off enough to let Uhl start making phone calls to Philadelphia, and he didn't want anybody down there any more alerted than they already were. And he didn't want Uhl on his back again coming down to Philadelphia in his wake.

On the other hand, he couldn't take the simple way out and kill Uhl here unless he was willing to kill Joyce Langer too, and so long as things weren't impossible otherwise, he wasn't willing to kill Joyce Langer. Her worst sin was stupidity combined with fluctuating emotionalism, and he didn't feel like doing anything about her except leaving her alone. And calling the building superintendent several hours from now, when this was all squared away, telling him to come up to this apartment to let her loose. If he didn't do that, considering how popular Joyce Langer seemed to be, she'd probably starve to death up here before anybody noticed she was missing.

The end result was that he had to take Uhl with him and finish the job somewhere on the road. Which was a little complicated, a little troublesome, but not impossible.

She had regained consciousness now. Parker saw her eyes open, saw her watching them walk through the living room. Uhl's head lolled, he shambled; he was obviously doped up. Over the gag around her mouth, her eyes were wide as she looked at Uhl.

They left the apartment and rode down in the elevator, Uhl leaning against the wall on the way down. They got out of the elevator on the first floor, and an old woman with a full shopping cart gave Uhl an odd look as she got aboard the elevator to go up.

Parker dropped Joyce Langer's key in the superintendent's mailbox, then led Uhl outside to where his car stood illegally close to a fire hydrant. There was a ticket on the windshield.

Uhl was still as docile as a lobotomized monk. Parker walked him around the car and settled him the passenger seat, then went around to the driver's side, plucked the ticket from the windshield and dropped it in the gutter, got in behind the wheel, and drove away from there.

Uhl quickly sagged against the door on his side. His eyes remained open, but he gave no indication of consciousness.

Parker went down the West Side Highway and through the Lincoln Tunnel and down the Jersey Turnpike from exit sixteen to exit fifteen, where he got off and took a lot of slumlike city streets until he wound up on a bumpy blacktop road past nothing but weeds. He was driving into a part of the Jersey swamp, where over the years a lot of things no longer wanted in New York have wound up. George Uhl wouldn't be the first man among them.

146

Parker stopped in a deserted area. The swamp was flat and green. Far away he could see bridges, factories, junkyards, oil refineries; but around here nothing but the flat green.

He got Uhl out of the car and walked him out across a soggy field through waist-high weeds. After a while he stopped and said, "Lie down," but when he let go of Uhl's arm Uhl just went limp and fell down, lying in a crumped heap in the weeds.

Parker took out his pistol and aimed it at Uhl's head, but he didn't fire.

It was stupid. There was no sense in it, and things without sense in them irritated him. Uhl was too docile, too easy. Somehow he was too much like a trusting child. Today or tomorrow he would wake up with a blinding headache and he would be again the guy who had twice tried to kill Parker, who had turned a very sweet job sour, who had killed his partners and stolen money that belonged to Parker, who had caused him trouble and discomfort of all kinds for five days in a row. That's who he'd been yesterday and that's who he'd be tomorrow, and Parker wouldn't think twice about exing that George Uhl out of the human race. But that wasn't who George Uhl was today. Today he was a docile child, and with angry irritation Parker realized that today he wasn't going to kill George Uhl.

But neither was he going to leave Uhl capable of getting back into the action. Nothing could make him quite that stupid. He put his pistol away again and bent over Uhl and broke three bones, all fairly important. Uhl groaned once and frowned, but that was all.

Parker walked back to the car and set off for Philadelphia.

Five

Twenty past one on a sunny spring Saturday afternoon in Philadelphia. Parker drove past Ed Saugherty's house, noticing the blue Datsun with New York plates parked out front, noticing the drapes wide open in the picture window. He went by without slowing, knowing they'd be watching, not wanting anybody on the inside to pay any particular attention to his car. They shouldn't be able to recognize him from over there; the house was set well back from the street.

The houses were widely spaced, but there was activity around more than half of them. Children rode bicycles, men mowed lawns or washed automobiles — all the weekend business of the straight world. Parker continued along the curving street until the Saugherty house was just out of sight in the rearview mirror but the blue Datsun could still be seen partway around the curve, and then he pulled to the curb and parked.

This was the worst possible place and the worst possible time for private business. If he parked here more than ten minutes the people in the neighboring houses would start to wonder about him, and within half an hour some busybody wife would send her husband out to smile at him in artificial friendliness and ask could he help, was Parker lost, was there anything in particular he wanted around here. But if he went away and waited till tonight to come back, Rosenstein and Brock might already be gone. It depended on how long it took them to squeeze the money out of Ed Saugherty. They didn't have it yet, which was lucky, but how long would Ed Saugherty hold out against a Matt Rosenstein and a Paul Brock?

But if he could neither go away and come back tonight nor stay here and keep them under surveillance, for many of the same reasons he couldn't break into the house right now. They would be on the alert in there, and green lawn spread out bright and empty on all four sides of the house. The houses were well separated here, and between Saugherty and his neighbors there were no hedges, no privacy fences, nothing but lawn. Parker wouldn't make it to the house alive, and a gun battle in the middle of a Saturday afternoon in this neighborhood wouldn't be the brightest idea in the world anyway.

Two boys on bicycles rode by, looking at him curiously.

He couldn't leave. He couldn't stay. He couldn't bull his way in.

Which left only one thing to do. He put the car in gear and drove three curving blocks before he found a telephone booth on a corner. He stopped the car, stepped into the booth, and dialed Saugherty's house.

Brock answered, and Parker said, "Hello, Brock, this is Parker. Put Rosenstein on."

All he got was a gasp.

"Come on, Brock, we're all in a hurry. Put your angel on, let's go."

Brock didn't say anything, but Parker heard the receiver thud down on a piece of furniture. He thought he could vaguely hear conversation going on far from the phone. He waited, and the next voice he heard was the same one that had questioned him that time at Brock's place:

"Parker?"

"Rosenstein?"

"Yeah. You the one called before?"

"Yes."

"Had us a little confused here. What's on your mind?"

"I've got Uhl," Parker said.

"That's good," Rosenstein said. "Have fun with him."

"I used that serum of yours on him."

There was a little pause, and Rosenstein said, "You did?"

"So now I know the situation," Parker said. "I know I need Saugherty."

Rosenstein laughed. "Ain't that the truth. Sorry, baby, he

149

isn't for sale."

"But you need Uhl," Parker told him.

Another little silence, and Rosenstein said, "How do you figure that?"

"You don't have the money, and you won't get it without Uhl. Just like I won't get it without Saugherty. You've got Saugherty. I've got Uhl."

"Are you talking deal?"

"Better we each get half than nobody gets anything."

"Maybe. Maybe I don't need Uhl at all."

"If you didn't," Parker said, improvising, "You'd have the money by now and be gone from there."

"If I had that damn serum—"

"You need Uhl."

"Hold on a minute."

Parker held on. He didn't know what Saugherty had done with the money, or why it was taking Rosenstein and Brock so long to get it out of him, but unless Saugherty fell apart in the next thirty seconds this idea ought to work.

Rosenstein came back. "Just for the sake of argument, what's on your mind?"

"Fifty-fifty split."

"I know that. How do you want to work it?"

"We'll meet and talk things over," Parker said, and knowing Rosenstein would object, he said, "We'll figure out some place we can meet, and—"

"You mean I leave here? That's damn likely, isn't it? Don't be stupid, Parker."

"All right then. You tell me."

"Just tell me what Uhl told you. We'll get the dough and leave you half. You're in the neighborhood, right?"

"I'm a few blocks away."

"In a phone booth on the corner? Yeah, I know that one. So just give me the story."

"And you'll leave me half," Parker said.

There was a little silence, and then Rosenstein chuckled. "It was worth a try," he said.

"We can't stall around forever," Parker said. "Neither of us is going to get more than half, so let's face it."

Rosenstein sighed. "All right. But I'm not leaving here."

"Then I don't know," Parker said. He wanted the suggestion to come from Rosenstein so he wouldn't be suspicious of it. It finally did. "Why don't you come here?" Rosenstein said. "We can work out a way you can come in without exposing yourself. I don't suppose you'll take my word for a safe conduct or anything."

"I won't."

"All right. Set it up any way you want."

Parker nodded, having gotten where he wanted to go. He said, "Is there a car in the garage?"

"What? Yeah."

"Remove it. Park it down by the curb and leave the garage door open. But neither you nor Brock is to be in the garage. I'll drive straight in. What room does the garage connect to?"

"The kitchen."

"Is there a table in there?"

"Yeah."

"You two be sitting at it with your hands where I can see them. You can leave the door to the garage open or shut, it's up to you. I'll come in empty-handed. You can have one gun on the table so you'll know I won't come in shooting."

"All right. What about Uhl?"

"He's in the trunk of my car. Don't worry, he's out of the play."

"Good. Anything else?"

"Not here."

"All right. We'll empty the garage for you."

"I'm on my way," Parker said.

Six

The garage was at the left end of the house, its door like an open mouth. Parker drove into it with no hands on the wheel, looking for the doorway that had to be somewhere in the right-side wall, the one leading into the kitchen. His left hand was on the door handle beside him, and his right hand had a revolver in it.

There was a slight blacktop slope up from the road, and then the flat garage floor. Parker went up, fast, into the garage too fast, stood on the brake at the last second, saw that interior doorway empty in the middle of the wall to his right, shoved the car door open with his shoulder, and went out of the car backwards, dropping toward the floor as the first bullet came from that doorway over there into the car through the windshield and out this side, six inches over Parker's head.

The car bumped into the rear wall. It was still in drive; the motor kept turning over, it kept pushing against the wall, but not hard enough to do any damage.

Parker hit the floor between the car and the exterior wall, folded his arms in close against his body, and rolled under the car. He kept himself rolling across the cement floor, the car rumbling over his head.

The garage door was sliding down. It must be run electrically, with a switch somewhere in the house.

Parker rolled out from under the right side of the car. Brock, startled, was standing in the doorway on the landing there with the open kitchen doorway on his right and the cellar stairs behind him. Parker had been in the garage less than ten seconds. He fired, lying on his back, and Brock jerked and toppled backwards down the cellar stairs.

Parker lunged for the wall as a shot was fired from the kitchen. It came through the angle of the two doorways and slapped into the side of the car.

The garage door was down. There'd been three shots, only one with the door open. With any luck the neighbors were all too busy and too far away to have noticed anything, but there couldn't be a lot of noise from here on.

Exhaust was beginning to stink up the garage already. The car engine was still growling, pushing against the rear wall of the garage.

There was a faint call from the cellar: "Matt! Help me, Matt!"

"Damn you, Parker!"

That was Rosenstein's voice from somewhere in the kitchen. Parker was pressed against the wall to the right of the doorway. There were two steps up to the doorway, and then the little landing inside and the kitchen doorway on the left.

There couldn't be a stalemate now. He had to keep moving, keep Rosenstein from getting himself reorganized. There was a pegboard mounted on the wall to Parker's right, the other way from the door, with tools hanging on it. He grabbed a hammer, stepped away from the wall so he could see on a diagonal through the two doorways into the kitchen, and threw the hammer at the far wall in there to give Rosenstein something else to think about for two seconds. He followed the hammer in, running low, diving across the threshold, firing blindly to his right as he went in. Not to hit anything, just to keep Rosenstein off balance, surround him with movement and noise.

A bullet ripped cloth above Parker's shoulder blade, and then he was on the floor, on his side. Rosenstein was in the doorway at the far end of the right-hand wall. Parker had two hands on the gun for stability, his arms were outstretched and he fired as Rosenstein dove out of the doorway. Rosenstein roared and crashed somewhere out of sight.

Was he hit? Parker was on his feet and running. He went fast around the corner and almost tripped over Rosenstein lying on the living room floor. Rosenstein was trying to bring his gun hand up. Parker kicked his wrist and the gun went sailing across

153

the room. Rosenstein grunted and fell back. His breathing sounded clogged but there was no blood visible.

Any more of them? Parker crouched over Rosenstein, looking around, but the house was full of silence.

Rosenstein was looking up at him. Talking as though his throat was closing up on him he said, "You broke my back."

Parker straightened. There'd been only the two of them. He went farther into the living room and picked up Rosenstein's pistol and put it in his hip pocket.

Rosenstein coughed and said, "You had luck. I could have taken you, but you had luck."

Parker walked back to him.

Rosenstein's eyes were red; they looked veiled. "I should have killed you when I had you," he said, his voice very thick now.

Parker reversed his gun and bent down and chopped once across Rosenstein's head.

Now to find Saugherty. He straightened, keeping the gun in his hand, and walked down the hall, opening doors. In one room was a woman, naked, tied and gagged and lying on a bed. She had bruises on her face and body, but she was conscious, and the one eye glaring at Parker looked wild. In another room three children in pajamas were tied and gagged and lying on beds. They moved like chipmunks when he opened the door. But in no room at all was there a man.

He went back to the living room. Rosenstein hadn't moved. He went through the kitchen and switched on the cellar light and saw Brock lying on the floor down there. Brock's head moved, and he called, "Matt?" His voice trembled.

Parker went down the stairs. He hunkered beside Brock and said, "Where's Saugherty?"

Brock's eyes had trouble finding him, and then he said, "You. You ruined my apartment."

"Where's Saugherty?" Parker said.

"Why did you break everything? You didn't have to break everything."

154

Parker took Brock by the shoulder and moved him. Brock gasped, his eyes widened, his face went white, and he looked as though he'd pass out. "Don't. I can't move like that, it hurts!"

"Then pay attention," Parker told him.

Brock blinked rapidly. He breathed in quick gulps and said, "Where's Matt?"

"Upstairs. He says he's got a broken back. The sooner I'm done here the sooner the both of you get a doctor. Where's Saugherty?"

Brock closed his eyes. "Dead," he said.

"Why?"

"He tried to fight Matt." Brock was talking now in a monotone, his eyes shut. "Matt went after his wife; he tried to — Matt got mad and wouldn't quit. I tried to get him to quit, but he just kept at the poor bastard. He wouldn't quit." He opened his eyes and said, "He's back in the other part of the cellar. On a glider back there."

"And the money?"

"The wife doesn't know anything. We asked her after you called the first time. Matt leaned on her a little, but she doesn't know anything. Just that Uhl called at dinnertime yesterday, and after he called Saugherty went out of the house with a suitcase and came back without it."

"She doesn't know where he went?"

"If she knew, she'd have told Matt. She really would."

Parker believed it. Saugherty hadn't told his wife where he'd hidden the money, and now Saugherty was dead, and that meant the money was gone for good. At least there was no way Parker would ever get his hands on it. If Saugherty had left the suitcase with a friend, which was more than likely what he'd done, the friend would probably sooner or later return it to Saugherty's widow. Or maybe look inside it and keep it for himself. Whatever happened in the future, though, was going to be way too late, and there was nothing to be done in the present. The money was gone.

"Well, you two really did it," Parker said and got to his feet again. "Good-bye, Brock," he said and started up the stairs.

Brock called after him, "Parker!"

Parker looked down at him.

"You're going to leave us to the law?"

"I'm doing better than that," Parker told him. "I'm going to leave you to Saugherty's wife."

Richard Stark is one of four pseudonyms of Donald Westlake (1933–2008), prolific author of noir crime fiction. Stark's short crime novels about an independent, hardworking criminal named Parker start with *The Hunter* (made into the film *Point Blank*) and end with *Butcher's Moon* (1974)—and then, after more than twenty years, revive with *Comeback* (1998), *Backflash* (1999), and six more, up to the latest, *Dirty Money* (2008). In 1993 the Mystery Writers of America bestowed the society's highest honor on Westlake, naming him a Grand Master. *Comeback* and *Backflash* were selected as *New York Times Notable Books of the Year*. In 2009, *The Hunter* was made into a graphic novel by Darwyn Cooke.